Once Upon a Time

윤동재 원작, 박정수 옮김

Once Upon a Time

발행일	2015년 8월 21일

지은이	윤 동 재		
옮긴이	박 정 수		
펴낸이	손 형 국		
펴낸곳	(주)북랩		
편집인	선일영	편집	서대종, 이소현, 이은지
디자인	이현수, 윤미리내, 임혜수	제작	박기성, 황동현, 구성우, 이탄석
마케팅	김회란, 박진관, 이희정, 김아름		
출판등록	2004. 12. 1(제2012-000051호)		
주소	서울시 금천구 가산디지털 1로 168, 우림라이온스밸리 B동 B113, 114호		
홈페이지	www.book.co.kr		
전화번호	(02)2026-5777	팩스	(02)2026-5747

ISBN   979-11-5585-704-5 03810 (종이책)   979-11-5585-705-2 05810 (전자책)

ONCE UPON A TIME

윤동재 원작 / 박정수 옮김

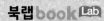
북랩 book Lab

Preface

The idea of translating a book and publishing it first came to my mind two years ago when I first started volunteering at an organization to translate letters to the children in developing countries from Korean to English. This experience helped me realize how passionate I was about translating and I felt like I was helping two distant people from different countries that speak different languages communicate and become one. This idea motivated me to translate a Korean children's story book to help people with similar backgrounds as me who are familiar with the traditions and culture of the country they were raised in, but not of their parents'.

Although I was born as a Korean, I grew up most of my life in Brazil. I grew up in Brazil for 13 years, and then I moved to Peru, where I lived for two years. Growing up in South America, I grew up reading Brazilian traditional children's story books and I grew up being familiar to the Brazilian culture. The Korean traditional children's story books and the culture seemed like a whole new world I didn't know of, very distant from me. So two years ago, during the vacation I moved to Korea, I read some Korean traditional story books to become familiar with my country and one of the books called, 「구비구비 옛이야기」 by 윤동재 really caught my eye. It seemed like the perfect children's book of stories where any reader could be able to sense the distinct Korean culture inside each story. This book was exactly the kind of book I was looking for. So I translated this book into English, Portuguese, and Spanish. The purpose of the book was definitely my passion for translating, but also to promote the Korean culture to as many people that I could reach through the book. With this translated book, I plan on donating several copies to the Korean churches I attended in Brazil and Peru. I hope to spread the Korean culture and help the Korean Brazilians and the Korean Peruvians become familiar with their parents' culture. I also hope to inform and help non-Korean Portuguese or Spanish speakers in South America become familiar with the Korean culture as well through this simple children's story book.

I hope that people become intrigued and fascinated by the Korean culture while reading the stories inside this book and I wish that this book is able to provide all readers with a better sense and familiarity of the Korean traditions and culture.

Lastly, I would like to thank the author of the book 「구비구비 옛이야기」, 윤동재, for giving me this opportunity to translate a book and help spread the Korean culture.

Thank you,
Jung Su Park

Contents

Preface / 04

Once Upon a Time - in English /13

The Rascal Who Impressed the Tiger / 14

The Calf Who Was Divided into Two / 16

The Nastiest Fly in the World / 18

The Mosquito and the Toad / 20

The Pregnant Bull / 22

Why the Toad has a Rounded Belly / 23

The Mischievous Groom / 24

In the Well / 26

Call It Muk Again / 28

Pine Needles / 30

Pretending to be Mutes / 31

Mr. Kim's Wife / 32

The Dumb Son in Law / 34

Why the Seawater is Salty / 36

The Spring Water / 38

God's Pee / 39

The Bedbug, the Flea, and the Louse / 40

Gyeongbokgung Palace / 42

The Croaker / 44

The Cost of the Rice Cake / 46

The Magpie Who Became Manly / 48

The Malicious Owner and the Servant's Son / 50

The Full Moon / 52

The First Time Mr. Lee Was Fooled / 54

Paektu Mountain and Halla Mountain / 56

Bragging Their Ages / 58

Andong's Official Mr. Kim's Servant / 60

I'm Also a Chestnut Tree / 62

The Man Who Was Chosen as the Administrator / 64

Let's Only Eat Rice Cake / 66

The Mute Daughter in Law / 68

The Rabbit / 70

The Partially Deaf People / 72

The Village School Teacher / 74

The Billionaire's Son and The Millionaire's Daughter / 76

Seorak Mountain's Cicadas / 78

Érase Una Vez - in Spanish /81

El Travieso que Impresionó el Tigre / 82

El Becerro Que Se Dividió en Dos / 84

La Mosca Más Desagradable en el Mundo / 86

El Mosquito y el Sapo / 88

El Toro Embarazada / 90

Por Qué el Sapo Tiene Una Barriga Redondeada / 91

El Novio Travieso / 92

En el Pozo / 94

Llámalo Muk de Nuevo / 96

Agujas de Pino / 98

Pretendiendo do Ser Mudos / 99

La Esposa de Señor Kim / 100

El Estúpido Yerno / 102

Por Qué El Agua del Mar es Salada / 104

El Agua de la Fuente / 106

La Orina del Dios / 107

La Chinche de Cama, la Pulga, y el Piojo / 108

El Palacio Gyeongbokgung / 110

La Corvina Amarilla / 112

El Costo de La Torta de Arroz / 114

La Marica que se Convirtió Viril / 116

El Dueño Malicioso y el Hijo del Sirviente / 118

El Plenilunio / 120

La Primera Vez Señor Lee Fue Engañado / 122

Monte Paektu y el Monte Halla / 124

Jactando Sus Edades / 126

El Sirviente del Oficial Señor Kim de Andong / 128

Yo También Soy Un Castaño / 130

El Hombre Que Fue Elegido Como el Administrador / 132

Vamos A Sólo Comer Torta de Arroz / 134

La Nuera Muda / 136

El Conejo / 138

La Gente Que Eran Parcialmente Sordas / 140

El Profesor de la Escuela del Pueblo / 142

El Hijo del Multimillonario e la Hija del Millonario / 144

Las Cigarras del Monte Seorak / 146

Era Uma Vez - in Portuguese /149

O Malandro que Impressionou o Tigre / 150

O Bezerro que Foi Dividido em Dois / 152

A Mosca Mais Desagradável do Mundo / 154

O mosquito e o Sapo / 156

O Touro Grávida / 158

Porque o Sapo tem Uma Barriga Arredondada / 159

O Noivo Travesso / 160

Dentro do Poço / 162

Chamá-lo Muk de Novo / 164

Agulhas de Pinheiro / 166

Fingindo de Ser Mudos / 168

A Esposa do Senhor Kim / 170

O Estúpido Genro / 172

Por Que a Água do Mar É Salgada / 174

A Água de Fonte / 176

O Xixi de Deus / 177

O Percevejo de Cama, a Pulga, e o Piolho / 178

O Palácio Gyeongbokgung / 180

A Corvina Amarela / 182

O Custo do Bolo de Arroz / 184

A Pêga Que se Tornou Viril / 186

O Dono Malicioso e o Filho do Servente / 188

O Plenilúnio / 190

A Primeira Vez Senhor Lee Foi Enganado / 192

Montanha Baekdu e a Montanha Halla / 194

Jactando Suas idades / 196

O Servente do Oficial Senhor Kim do Andong / 198

Eu Também Sou Um Castanheiro / 200

O Homem Que Foi Escolhido Como o Administrador / 202

Vamos só Comer Bolo de Arroz / 204

A Nora Muda / 206

O Coelho / 208

As Pessoas Que Eram Parcialmente Surdas / 210

O Professor da Escola da Aldeia / 212

O Filho do Bilionário e A Filha do Milionário / 214

As Cigarras da Montanha Seorak / 216

Once Upon a Time
in English

The Rascal Who Impressed the Tiger

There was a rascal who

Didn't go to the bathroom when he had to pee in the middle of

the night

But instead went to go pee in the kitchen

The Kitchen God

Couldn't put up with the smell of urine anymore

And asked the Mountain God to scold the little devil

The Mountain God who had received the Kitchen God's favor

Called the tiger who is good at running errands

And asked him this,

"If you go downtown, there is a rascal who pees in the kitchen.

Go there and blow him out of the water for me!"

The tiger came down to the village

And hid behind the rascal's back yard

He hid there remaining still

In the middle of the night,

The rascal really did enter the kitchen

And peed babbling

The tiger stood up to scold the naughty boy

But the boy started to mumble to himself

The tiger perked his ears to listen to the boy and heard him say,

"If I'm freezing even when I'm confined in my house,

how cold the tiger in the mountains must be!"

After the tiger heard the rascal speak,

He decided he couldn't scold

A rascal who loved him so much and

Went back to the mountains

He decided it would be better for him to be scolded by the

Mountain God

And went back up to the mountains

The Calf Who Was Divided into Two

In a village called Gyeongju in the Gyeonsang District,

A farmer was feeding another person's cow

It was pregnant so it had a bulging stomach

The cow finally calved

And gave birth to two calves at the same time

The farmer wanted

One of the two calves for himself

So, he went to the neighboring village to find the owner of the
cow

And didn't tell him the cow gave birth to two calves

But said there was only one calf

After listening to the farmer, the owner of the cow said,

"You could've just said the cow gave birth to a calf instead of
one calf

That is very strange, that is very strange

They said my cow would always give birth to two calves at the same time."

And then the farmer said honestly

"I guess there's another cow that gives birth to two calves at the same time."

Then, the owner of the cow smiled and said

"Giving birth to two calves means to share the calves."

And gave one calf to the farmer

The Nastiest Fly in the World

An old miser called Jung, who lives in Chungju,

Was eating lunch on the field

With only one small dish of soy sauce and

A bowl of boiled barley

After doing farm work on a boiling hot summer day

But as he ate a spoon of boiled barley

And was about to dip into the soy sauce,

A fly descended and sat down on the small dish of soy sauce

And coated its hind leg with soy sauce

And quickly escaped

Old mister Jung

Followed the fly,

Saying he would find his precious soy sauce again

And after running 500m to Mungyeong Saejae Pass,

He finally caught the fly

And then,

He blasted away the fly saying,

"You nasty fly!"

And sucked the soy sauce on the fly's hind leg

And then released it

The Mosquito and the Toad

Once upon a time, there was a mosquito and a toad

Who lived in the countryside

They decided to have a competition

And see who could go to

Namdaemun[1] in Seoul first

The mosquito secretly thought,

'There's no point in competing

Because I'm obviously going to win anyway

Since I can obviously fly and

The toad is going to have to crawl all the way there.'

But after actually doing it,

It wasn't as easy as the mosquito had thought

Rain or shine,

The toad slowly crawled along

---

1) The Great South Gate in Seoul

But after actually competing,

It wasn't as easy as he had thought

When it was windy or raining

The mosquito couldn't fly

And because of that,

The toad got to Namdaemun in Seoul first

And when the mosquito got there several days later,

The toad put on a haughty attitude, boasted and said,

"Ahem, ahem. Look.

The straw shoes I was sitting on completely rotted."

The Pregnant Bull

Dolse, Mr. Kim's 7 year old son,
Went looking for lord Hong
And asked him, "Lord, lord. My dad had a
Healthy baby boy today
And we don't have any seaweed in our house.
Can you please give us some?"

After hearing that, Lord Hong laughed outright and said,
"Oh, little boy. How can a man give birth to a child?"
But the boy didn't yield and said,
"Lord, lord. Where is the pregnant bull?"

Then, Lord Hong remembered
Recently telling Mr. Kim
That he'd be scolded
If he didn't bring Hong the pregnant bull
And feeling shameful, said,
"I'm sorry,
I'm sorry."
To the little boy

Why the Toad has a Rounded Belly

One day, the fox, the rabbit, and the toad
Made rice cake and decided that
The person who is worst at holding liquor
Would have to eat all the rice cake

The rabbit was the first one to happily accept
And step up and said, "I get drunk just by going near a wheat
field."
The fox said, "I get drunk just by looking at the drunk rabbit's
face."

The toad didn't say anything
When the rabbit and the fox asked why he wasn't saying a word,
The toad said, "I'm already drunk just by listening to you guys
That I can't talk."

And said the person who is worst at holding liquor is him
And ate all the rice cake
And this is why
The toad has a rounded belly

The Mischievous Groom

In the Joseon Dynasty,

Song Si-Yeol lord was a famous mischief-maker when he was

young

At the wedding ceremony, the bride isn't allowed to talk

But when his friends asked him to do a bet,

To see if he could get the bride to talk at the wedding,

The groom was full of confidence

So on the day he was getting married, he went in the wedding

And it was his turn to bow down to the bride

But he didn't bow down on purpose and just stood there

"Bow down. Quickly, quickly." People told him

But he just stood there stiffly

When people asked why he was standing there like that

He said, "My grandma is a mute

My mother is a mute

And if my bride is also a mute, I am never going to get married."

And told the bride to say something

The bride wasn't supposed to talk in the wedding ceremony

But just had to after hearing what the groom said

And because the bride talked at the wedding ceremony,

The groom Song Si-Yeol won the bet with his friends

And thanks to the bride, was treated with a nice meal from his friends

In the Well

In a stream with no water,

There was a fish floundering and saying,

"Please save me, please save me!"

A blind person saw that and yelled,

"Help, help!

There's a fish floundering here!"

A deaf person heard this and said,

"Anybody there? Anybody there?

Somebody please come and scoop this fish out!"

A crippled person came running and said he'd rescue the fish

A monk wearing a top-knot came running first

And rescued the fish

And while running up and down

Shouting "The fish is now alive!"

The fish splashed into the well

People gathered to look into the well

But there was no fish

Only lies floating around

Only lies floating around

Call It Muk Again

During the war, the king fled

And was eating a meal at a farmer's house

The fish on the royal table was so good that

The king asked the farmer what the name of the fish was

The farmer said, "The fish is called muk[2]."

The king said, "Why would you name such a delicious fish like that?"

And told the farmer to name it Sweetfish

After the war, the king returned to the royal palace

And ate the fish on the royal table

And said, "This tastes horrible. This tastes horrible.

What is the name of the fish?"

---

[2]   A Korean food made from grains, beans, or nut starch such as buckwheat, sesame, and acorn and has a jelly-like consistency

The famer said, "The fish is called Sweetfish."

The king said, "Why would you name such a horrible fish like that?"

And told the farmer to name it muk again

Pine Needles

The Paektu Mountain[3] God and the dragon King of the East Sea
Decided to meet each other on Jongno street
To compare and see who had more possessions

The Paektu Mountain God said
All grass and trees are his
And the dragon King of the East Sea said
All fish are his

While they were counting together to see who had more
possessions,
The Paektu Mountain God thought
There'd be a less number of grass and trees
And decided to play a trick

He ripped off whole pine needles
One by one and quickly increased the number of leaves
And barely tied with the dragon King of the East Sea

---

3)   An active volcano located on the border of China and North Korea

Pretending to be Mutes

Three friends gathered together
And agreed to
Scrounge for a meal
By acting like mutes

When lunchtime came,
They went to the front of a wealthy family's gate
And stood still
Lunchtime passed
And yet no one came out to give them food

One of the three of them shouted,
"Give me some food, please!"
Another one scolded him for speaking
When they had agreed to pretend to be mutes

The other friend bragged to the two
And he said, "I'm different from you guys.
I'm going to be a good mute
And not say a single word."

Mr. Kim's Wife

Mr. Kim lives with his old father

And his wife mistreats him day and night

That always bothered him

So Mr. Kim decided to use a trick and told his wife,

"Honey, I went to the market and

You can sell a fat old man at a high price."

After hearing that,

The wife thought, 'It'd be great if we could fatten up

The father in law and sell him.'

And treated her father in law nicely

The father in law was happy because he was

Getting along with his daughter in law

He told stories to his grandchildren, looked after their studies

And even fetched water for the daughter in law

And put it in the kitchen

After much time had passed,

Mr. Kim said to his wife,

"Honey, lets sell my father at the market now."

Mr. Kim's wife flew into a rage and yelled,

"No way! That's not happening!"

The Dumb Son in Law

A long time ago, a house got a son in law

And the father in law thought he was very stupid

The father in law decided he couldn't leave the son in law alone

And made him learn letters

The father in law told him,

"All you have to do is

Copy what I do.

It's a mere child's play.

Since I'm the father in law, I will start first."

The son in law even followed the "I will start first."

And when the father in law said, "Copy me without saying

The 'I will start first' part."

The son in law even followed the "Copy me without saying

The 'I will start first' part."

The father in law thought there was no hope in teaching letters to this fellow

When the father in law said, "Old bean, just give up."

The son in law even followed the "Just give up."

He bravely followed the "Just give up."

Why the Seawater is Salty

Once upon a time, there was a millstone that popped out
anything you asked for

When you say, "Come out rice." and spin the millstone, rice
would come out

When you say, "Come out money." and spin the millstone,
money would come out

Whey you say, "Come out clothes" and spin the millstone,
clothes would come out

When you say, "Come out salt" and spin the millstone, salt
would come out

When you say, "Come out meat" and spin the millstone, meat
would come out

When you say, "Come out fruits" and spin the millstone, fruits
would come out

A thief who somehow found out about this millstone stole it,

Loaded it on his boat and was on his way

When he said, "Come out salt" and spun the millstone

All of a sudden, salt gushed out continuously

And flooded the boat and didn't stop there

The boat sank into the sea with the millstone

To this day, the millstone continues to spin, gushing out salt

And there still is no one who knows how to stop the millstone

This is why the seawater is salty and it continues to be salty

The Spring Water

In the Joseon Dynasty, there was an old man
Who lived near Mt. Kumgang[4]
One day, he carried an A-frame[5] on his back and
Went to go cut wood in the mountains
After cutting a load of trees, he became thirsty
And drank from the spring
But that water was no ordinary water
So after the old man took a sip of water,
He became a young man again, a broth of a man

After seeing the grandpa return home as a young man,
The grandma was so jealous
That she followed him to go cut woods the next day
And drank the spring water first even though she wasn't thirsty
But the grandma drank way too much water
That she became a baby
And the grandpa didn't recognize her
He never ever recognized again who the baby was

---

4) Also known as Geumgang Mountain, it is one of the most famous mountains in
North Korea (Kangwon-do)
5) Korean traditional back carrier

God's Pee

Once upon a time,

God descended to the top of Paektu Mountain

And started looking for places to pee because he needed to pee

But he just couldn't find a place to pee

So he ended up peeing

On top of Paektu Mountain

Thus, the top of Paektu Mountain

Was dug deeply and became the Heaven Lake

And the water that flooded east

Became the Tumen River, which flows to this day

And the water that flooded west

Became the Yalu River, which flows to this day

The Bedbug, the Flea, and the Louse

The bedbug, the flea, and the louse are siblings
The bed bug, the eldest brother
The flea, the second oldest brother
And the louse, the youngest brother

The bedbug and the flea
Don't listen to their parents
And drink day and night
The louse studies hard

One day, the bedbug and the flea drank
And got into a quarrel
The louse told the brothers
"Brothers, don't fight!"
and tried to stop the fight

But he was pushed hard and fell on the ground

And was bruised with a black and blue mark on his back

Bedbug and Flea started to feel tipsy

And turned red all over

So Louse's back is still black and blue

Bedbug is red all over

And Flea is red all over

Gyeongbokgung Palace

There was a Buddhist monk called Muhak,

Who helped the first king of the Joseon Dynasty, Yi Seong-Gye

When Muhak was building the Gyeongbokgung Palace,

He noticed it kept collapsing if he built it here

So he went around here and there

To build it somewhere else

One day, he went to to a place

And a farmer was plowing the fields while driving a cattle

But the cattle kept acting up to the farmer

And didn't plow the fields well

So the farmer laid into the cattle and said,

"Ugh this cow! You're stupid just like Muhak!"

Muhak, the Buddhist monk, feigned innocence

And asked, "How come Muhak is stupid?"

The farmer said, "The place called Hanyang⁶⁾ is shaped like a heron

So the four main gates of Seoul have to be built first to fix the wings of the heron

And then build the Gyeongbokgung Palace

But Muhak doesn't know how to do that so isn't he stupid?"

After listening to the farmer, Muhak said,

"That's true.

That's definitely true."

And built the four main gates of Seoul first

And then built the Gyeongbokgung Palace later

After that, Gyeongbokgung Palace actually never collapsed again

---

6) The capital of Joseon, currently known as Seoul

The Croaker

Mr. Park, the old miser from Jinju[7]
Drew a croaker and hung it on the ceiling
And every time his family ate dinner,
He made them scoop a spoon full of rice,
Look at the drawing once,
And then eat their meal

His family said,
"If you're going to make us eat
With a drawing of a croaker,
You could have as well just drawn
Two
Or three croakers instead."

---

7) A city in Gyeongsang (South) province

What was even worse was when

He severely scolded his family

"Eat just a little. East just a little.

You might have to drink a lot of water."

When they accidentally stared at the drawing

For just a little too long

The Cost of the Rice Cake

A rice cake[8] merchant was selling rice cakes

He left his seat for a second

And all the rice cakes were gone

The rice cake merchant ran to the magistrate

And told him he had lost all the rice cakes he was selling

And asked him to find them

The magistrate called everyone over

And gave them each a cup of water

And told them, "This water is medicine

So do not swallow it.

Put it in your mouth

And then spit it out again."

---

8)   A traditional Korean food

Everyone did as they were told

And all took a sip of water and spat it out

And then the magistrate looked at each spit

And one by one found everyone

Who had the scraps of rice cakes in their spit

And made them pay for the cost of the rice cakes

The Magpie Who Became Manly

A fox looked up at a magpie's nest and said to the magpie,

"If you give me one of your chicks I will not kill you."

The magpie was scared of the fox

And so she gave one of her chicks to the fox

After eating a magpie chick, the fox again said,

"If you give me one of your chicks I will not kill you."

The magpie was scared of the fox

And so she gave another one of her chicks to the fox

The magpie trembled with fear

A heron was passing by and asked, "What's wrong?"

The magpie said, "It's because of the fox

The fox is so scary I can't bear it anymore."

Then the carne said to the magpie,

"The fox can't climb trees so

When the fox comes, tell him imposingly,

To try climbing up the tree."

The fox returned and said to the magpie,

"If you give me one of your chicks I will not kill you."

This time, the magpie wasn't scared of the fox and said

imposingly,

"I dare you to try climbing up the tree."

The fox struggled to climb up the tree several times

But he just glared and went back

He was never able to climb up the tree

And he just glared and went back

The Malicious Owner and the Servant's Son

Once upon a time,

A malicious owner

Told his house servant

To go to the mountains

And pick raspberries

Even though it was cold winter

After listening to the owner,

The servant didn't know what to do

So his son went to the owner and asked,

"My dad went to go pick raspberries in the mountains

And got bitten by a snake. This is terrible!

What medicine do I use?"

The owner said,

"There's no snake in the cold winter."

The servant's son talked back and said,

"There's no raspberries in this cold winter either!"

The owner took a hint and said,

"Let's pretend I never told someone to go pick raspberries."

The Full Moon

Once upon a time, in a county,

There was a dumb magistrate

It was the last day of the month, so there was no moon in the sky

The dumb magistrate got worried and called the administrator

The administrator said to the stupid magistrate,

"The moon was bought with money and hung above the sky

So that the county people could go around during the night too.

A magistrate bought it and hung it above the sky."

The stupid magistrate asked the administrator

How much he had to pay to buy the moon

The administrator told the stupid magistrate,

"You only have to pay 2000 Nyang[9] to buy the moon."

---

9) A unit of old Korean coinage

On the following evening, the administrator told the magistrate,

"Look! I bought the moon and hung it above the sky."

The stupid magistrate looked up to the sky

And saw the crescent moon hanging

He said the moon was too small and useless

The administrator told the stupid magistrate it was because

the moon's price rose a lot

The magistrate told the administrator he should buy the big moon

Even though it costs a lot of money

A few days later,

The administrator bought the big moon with ten thousand Nyang

And hung it above the sky

And told the stupid magistrate to look at the sky

The full moon was hanging above the sky

The First Time Mr. Lee Was Fooled

Mr. Lee always bragged that
He had never been fooled by anyone his entire life
One very cold winter day, a friend came to visit him
And told him, "I saw a cherry the size of a watermelon
On a cherry tree on my way here."

After hearing that, Mr. Lee said,
"There's no such thing as a cherry the size of a watermelon.
I'm not falling for that. I'm never falling for that!"
But the friend said,
"I saw it with my own eyes!
I even saw a cherry the size of a melon."

After hearing that, Mr. Lee said,
"There's no such thing as a cherry the size of a Korean melon
I'm not falling for that. I'm never falling for that!
I mean it'd be believable if
It were the size of a peach or a plum."

Then, the friend said,

"Have you really never been fooled by anyone before?

Then I fooled you for the first time.

How would a cherry grow in this freezing winter?

Ha-ha-ha!"

And laughed out loud. He dissolved into laughter.

Paektu Mountain and Halla Mountain

A long, long, very long time ago

Grandpa Paektu

Ate jujubes

And always threw the seeds

To one place

The seeds piled and piled and piled up

And became a mountain

Since then,

People named the mountain after the grandpa

And called it Paektu Mountain

A long, long, very long time ago

Grandpa Halla

Always threw a Go[10] stone

To one place

Every time the land and sea were reversed

The seeds piled and piled and piled up

And became a mountain

Since then,

People named the mountain after the grandpa

And called it Halla Mountain

---

10) Go ("encircling game") is a Korean board game similar to chess

Bragging Their Ages

Once upon a time,

The tiger, the fox, and the toad

Each argued that they were older than each other

The tiger first said, "I was born in the ancient times

Of the Japanese emperor."

Then, the fox said, "I was born during Shennong's[11] ruling."

But the toad didn't say anything

And just shed big drops of tears

The tiger and the fox

Said to the toad,

"So you're crying because

You were born last right?"

But the toad told them,

"That's absolutely not the reason.

I'm crying because

---

11) Shennong is also known as The Emperor of the Five Grains and was a legendary
ruler of China

I suddenly remembered

My eldest son who was born during the

Ancient times of the Japanese emperor

And my second son who was born during

Shennong's ruling

After listening to the toad,

The tiger and the fox were embarrassed

To have ever bragged about their ages

In front of the toad

And begged for mercy and said,

"Grandpa toad,

Please forgive us,

Please forgive us."

Andong's Official Mr. Kim's Servant

Official Mr. Kim, who lived in Andong,
Was going to Seoul with his servant
He became really hungry
And told his servant to go buy him
A bowl of soup

The servant bought the bowl of soup
But he kept fumbling in his pockets
On his way back
When Official Mr. Kim asked him
What he was fumbling in his pockets,

The servant answered,
"I dropped a sleep in the soup
On my way here
And I was just looking for it.

But the oil looks like sleep

And the sleep looks like oil too

So it's impossible to find it.

This is terrible!"

After hearing that, Official Mr. Kim

Lost his appetite

And told the servant to

Throw away the soup

Or eat it

Or do whatever he wants

After hearing that, the servant thought,

"Yes! Hooray!"

And ate the bowl of soup in a jiffy

I'm Also a Chestnut Tree

Professor Lee Yulgok from the Joseon Dynasty
Was destined to be bitten by a tiger
Someone once said, "If you plant one thousand
Chestnut trees you won't be bitten by a tiger."
So his family had planted one thousand chestnut trees

But one day, while Lee Yulgok was playing alone at home,
A tiger came and said, "Let's count together how many
chestnut trees are planted in your house!"

One tree, two trees, three trees
They counted the trees together
When something big happened
There were only 999 chestnut trees
There was exactly one tree
Missing from the 1000 trees

The tiger opened his mouth wide and said,

"Since there's one chestnut tree missing

From the planted trees here,

I'm going to eat you!"

And flew at Professor Lee Yulgok

But then, Professor Lee Yulgok waved his hands and said,

"Look! I'm also a chestnut tree! I'm also a chestnut tree!"

After hearing that, the tiger said,

"Oh okay! Then there are exactly 1000 trees! There are 1000

trees!"

And went back up to the mountains

The Man Who Was Chosen as the Administrator

A long time ago, in a county in Daegu,

The new magistrate from Seoul came

And four people volunteered to be the administrator

The new magistrate contemplated on whom

He should choose as his administrator

And decided he would pick the one who

Could guess his tough question

As his administrator

The new magistrate exerted himself and

Came up with a question,

"How many mountains are there in Daegu?"

Mr. Lee answered, "That's more than I can answer

Since there are more than one or two mountains here."

Mr. Kim answered, "There's Palgong Mountain, Biseul

Mountain,

And Duryu Mountain."

Mr. Park answered, "There's a big mountain and a small

mountain."

And lastly, Mr. Hong answered, "There are

A total of four mountains in Daegu.

In spring, there's the flower mountain,

In summer, there's the green mountain,

In fall, there's the maple mountain,

And in winter, there's the white mountain."

After listening to Mr. Hong, the new magistrate thought,

'Yes, that's it!' and chose Mr. Hong as his administrator

Let's Only Eat Rice Cake

A thrifty millionaire who didn't know
How to make rice cake at all
Had a daughter in law
One day, the daughter in law asked
Why he never made rice cake
The millionaire simply replied,
"It's just a loss to make rice cake."

After listening to the millionaire,
The daughter in law soaked three doe[12] of rice
In front of the millionaire
And swelled the rice so that it looked like
There were six doe of rice
And showed it to the millionaire again

---

12) A Korean unit of measure

After looking at it, the thrifty millionaire said,

"I guess it's not a loss to make rice cake.

My dear, let's make rice cake. Let's make rice cake."

The daughter in law made rice cake adding

Adzuki bean paste and gave it to the thrifty millionaire

The thrifty millionaire ate the rice cake and said,

"Let's not eat rice anymore.

Dear, let's only eat rice cake. Let's only eat rice cake.

It's so delicious and besides, there's no loss in making it.

Let's only eat rice cake."

The Mute Daughter in Law

A long time ago, when a young lady
Was getting married, her dad admonished her
By saying, "Dear, when you're married,
Live 9 years like this: Three years as a mute,
Three years as a deaf person,
And three years as a blind person."

The young lady never talked after she got married
She only talked in gestures
Unable to bear the young lady,
The father in law called his servants
And told them to take her back to her parents

The servants carried the young lady
On a palanquin back to her parents
But while they passed a pine grove
They let her out of the palanquin
So that she could pee

She saw a pheasant sitting in the pine grove

And said, "I wish I could catch that pheasant

And make a side dish out of it

For my father in law."

After hearing that, the servants put her in the palanquin again

And took her back to her father in law

And they told him that she had talked

He became delighted and started dancing

He danced joyfully

The Rabbit

A hunter went hunting and saw a rabbit

And shot it in the leg

The rabbit darted off with a limp

A town dog was walking along the mountain path

When he saw the rabbit darting off with a limp

He ran to it and snapped it

And took it home

The hunter hurriedly followed the dog

There was only a seven year old

Inside the house

The hunter told her to give back his rabbit

And the young girl said calmly and orderly,

"The one that made the rabbit's leg limp is you

But it was for sure my dog who caught the rabbit

And since you need the rabbit skin and

My dog needs the meat

You can take the rabbit skin and

We'll give my dog the rabbit meat."

The Partially Deaf People

A long time ago, in a house in Gyeongsang district
There lived a partially deaf daughter in law,
A partially deaf mother in law, and a partially deaf servant

One day, the daughter in law was in the kitchen
And said she'd make breakfast
And started preparing side dishes
While beating on the cutting board

The mother in law didn't even hear the noise clearly
And said from the bedroom,
"Dear, what are you saying?
Don't blame it on me!"

The daughter in law didn't even hear the mother in law clearly
And said from the kitchen,
"You're scolding me again today
For something that happened three days ago!"

The servant didn't even hear the daughter in law clearly

And said from the garden,

"You're still scolding me

For breaking the chamber pot by accident two months ago!"

The Village School Teacher

The village school teacher was teaching
A Chinese characters primer
But no matter how much he taught the dumb student,
The student didn't understand
So the teacher calmly told the student,
"I think it'd be better for you to sell fish instead of studying.
Go to large gathering places and just say, 'buy fish!'"

The dumb student did as he was told
And went to a large gathering place and said, "Buy fish!"
But it turned out to be a gathering to mourn the loss of an old
man
People got mad and scolded him,
"Where do you think you're selling fish!"

The dumb student went to his teacher and told him,

"I only did as you said and got scolded."

After listening to the student, the teacher

Patted the student on the shoulder and calmly told him again,

"When you go to places like that, you have to first ask people,

'Are you okay?'"

The dumb student said, "Very well, sir." And went

To a large gathering place and this time, asked people,

"Are you okay?"

But it turned out to be a gathering to celebrate

An old man's 70th birthday

People got mad and scolded him,

"Where do you think you're asking people if they're okay!"

The Billionaire's Son and The Millionaire's Daughter

One day, the billionaire

Asked his daughter in law,

Who was the millionaire's daughter

"Do you know how to set the table?"

"I don't know, sir."

"Do you know how to weave cloth?"

"I don't know, sir."

"Do you know how to sew garments?"

"I don't know, sir."

Whenever someone asked something,

She always said,

"I don't know, I don't know."

One day, the millionaire

Asked his son in law,

Who was the billionaire's son

"Do you know how to cut wood?"

He immediately went to the mountains

And came back with a load of logs

"Do you know how to make straw sandals?"

He immediately made a pair of straw sandals

"Do you know how to chop firewood?"

He immediately chopped a pile of firewood

There wasn't a task he couldn't do

There wasn't anything he couldn't do

Seorak Mountain's Cicadas

A long long time ago, there were no cicadas

In Seorak Mountain

How come there are so many cicadas now?

It's because they all came from Ulsan

There was a daoshi[13] living in Ulsan

And all he did all day was eat and sleep

One summer, the cicadas

Were crying too loudly

That the daoshi couldn't sleep

So he decided to make the cicadas mute

And tried to curse them and blow away all the cicadas

---

13) A priest in Taoism

But the cicadas were very crafty

And sensed what the daoshi was going to do

And flew all the way to Seorak Mountain to avoid the curse

And since then,

There were cicadas living in Seorak Mountain as well

Érase Una Vez

in Spanish

El Travieso que Impresionó el Tigre

Hubo un travieso

Que no ir al baño

Cuando tenía que hacer pis en medianoche

Pero en lugar, se fue a hacer pis en la cocina

El dios de la cocina

No podia aguantar el olor de la orina más

Y pidió al dios de la montaña a regañar al pequeño diablo

El dios de la montaña, que había recibido el favor del dios de la cocina

Llamó el tigre que es bueno en hacer mandados

E dijo esto,

"Si vas al centro, hay un travieso que hace pis en la cocina.

Ve allí reprenderlo severamente por mí!"

El tigre llegó a la aldea

Y se escondió detrás del patio del travieso

Se escondió allí, permaneciendo sin moverse

En medio de la noche,

El travieso realmente entró en la cocina

Y se orinó murmurando

El tigre se levantó para regañar al niño travieso

Pero el chico empezó a murmurar para sí mismo

El tigre se animó a sus oídos para escuchar al niño y le oyó

decir,

"Si me estoy congelando incluso cuando estoy confinado en mi

casa,

El tigre debe estar muy frío!"

Después de oír el travieso hablar,

El tigre decidió que no podía regañar

Un travieso que lo amaba tanto

Y regresó a las montañas

Él decidió que sería mejor para él ser reprendido por el dios de

la montaña

Y regresó a las montañas

El Becerro Que Se Dividió en Dos

En un pueblo llamado Gyeongju en el distrito Gyeonsang

Un granjero estaba alimentando la vaca de otra persona

Ella estaba embarazada, y así tenía un barriga protuberante

La vaca finalmente dio a luz

Y dio a luz a dos becerros al mismo tiempo

El granjero quería

Uno de los dos becerros para él mismo

Entonces, se fue a la aldea cercana para encontrar al dueño de la

vaca

Y no le dijo que la vaca dio a luz a dos becerros

Pero dijo que sólo había un becerro

Después de escuchar el granjero, el dueño de la vaca dijo,

"Podrías haber solamente decir que la vaca dio a luz al becerro

en lugar de un becerro.

Eso es muy extraño, es muy extraño.

Dijeron que mi vaca siempre daría a luz a dos becerros al mismo

tiempo."

Y despues, el granjero dijo honestamente,

"Yo creo que hay una otra vaca que da a luz a dos becerros al mismo tiempo."

Depues, el dueño de la vaca sonrió y dijo,

"Dar a luz a dos becerros significa para compartir los becerros."

Y dio un becerro para al granjero

La Mosca Más Desagradable en el Mundo

Un viejo avaro llamado Jung, quien vive en Chungju,

Estaba almorzando en el campo

Con sólo un pequeño plato de salsa de soya

Y un tazón de cebada cocida después de hacer

El trabajo en el campo en un día verano de calor sofocante

Pero mientras comía una cucharada de cebada hervida

Y estaba a punto de sumergirse en la salsa de soya,

Una mosca descendió y se sentó en el pequeño plato de salsa de

soya

Y mojó sus pierna

Y escapó rápidamente

El viejo avaro Jung

Siguió la mosca,

Diciendo que encontraría su preciosa salsa de soya de nuevo

Y después de corer 500m a Mungyeong Saejae Pass,

Él finalmente capturó la mosca

Y luego,

Reprendió la mosca diciendo,

"Su mosca desagradable!"

Y chupó la salsa de soya en la pata trasera de la mosca

Y luego, liberó la mosca

El Mosquito y el Sapo

Érase una vez, hubo un mosquito y un sapo

Que vivían en el campo

Ellos decidieron tener un competición

Y ver quién podía ir a

Namdaemun[14] en Seúl primero

El mosquito secretamente pensaba,

'No hay ningún punto en la competencia

porque obviamente voy a ganar de todas formas,

cómo obviamente puedo volar y

el sapo tendrá que avanzar a cuatro patas todo el camino hasta

allí.'

Pero después de hacerlo en realidad,

No fue tan fácil como el mosquito había pensado

Lluvia o sol,

---

14)   El Gran Puerta del Sur en Seúl

El sapo se arrastró lentamente hacia delante

Pero después de competir en realidad,

No era tan fácil como el mosquito había pensado

Cuando había viento o llueve

El mosquito no podía volar

Y debido a eso,

El sapo llegué al Namdaemun en Seúl primero

Y cuando el mosquito llegó varios días después,

El sapo se puso una actitud de gran arrogancia, alardeó, y dijo,

"Ahem, ahem. Mira.

Las sandalias de paja que estoy sentado en están completamente

podrido."

El Toro Embarazada

Dolse, el hijo de siete años del Señor Kim,

Fue a buscar a su Excelencia, Señor Hong

Y le preguntó, "Mi padre dio a luz a un bebé sano hoy

Y nosotros no tenemos alga marina en nuestra casa.

¿Podría darnos un poco de algas?

Después de escuchar eso, Señor Hong se rio a carcajadas y dijo,

"Ay, chiquito. ¿Cómo puede un hombre dar a luz a un niño?"

Pero el chico no dio y le dijo,

"Señor, señor. ¿Dónde está el toro embarazada?"

Y luego, el señor Hong recordó recientemente diciendo

El Señor Kim que iba a ser reprendido

Si él no trajo Hong un toro embarazada

Y sintiendo vergüenza, dijo,

"Lo siento mucho,

Lo siento."

Para el niño

Por Qué el Sapo Tiene Una Barriga Redondeada

Un día, el zorro, el conejo, y el sapo
hicieron un torta de arroz y decidieron que
La persona que es peor en el consumo de alcohol
Tendría que comer todo el torta de arroz

El conejo fue el primero para aceptar alegremente
Y dijo, "Me emborracho solamente por ir cerca de un campo de
trigo."
Y el sapo dijo, "Me emborracho con sólo mirar a la cara del
conejo borracho."

El sapo no dijo nada
Cuando el conejo y el zorro preguntaron por qué no decía
ninguna palabra,
El sapo dijo, "Yo ya estoy borracho con sólo escuchar a ustedes
Que no puedo hablar."

Y dijo que la persona que es peor en tomando alcohol es el
Y se comió toda la torta de arroz
Y esta es la razón
Que el sapo tiene una barriga redondeada

El Novio Travieso

En la dinastía Joseon,

El Milord Song Si-Yeol era un famoso juguetón cuando era joven

En la ceremonia de la boda, la novia no se le permite hablar

Pero cuando sus amigos le pidieron que hiciera una apuesta,

Para ver si podía hacer la novia hablar en la boda,

El novio estaba lleno de confianza

Así que el día en que el novio se iba a casar, él entró en la boda

Y era su turno para saludar la novia

Pero él no postrarse delante de ella a propósito y se quedó allí

"Saludarla. Rápido, rápido." La gente le dijeron

Pero él se quedó rígidamente

Cuando la gente le preguntaba por qué estaba allí de pie

Él dijo, "Mi abuela es un muda

Mi madre es un muda

Y si mi novia también es un muda, Nunca voy a casar."

Y dijo a la novia para decir algo

La novia no debía hablar en la ceremonia de la boda

Pero sólo tenía que después de escuchar lo que dijo el novio

Y porque la novia habló en la ceremonia de la boda,

El novio Song Si-Yeo ganó la apuesta con sus amigos

Y gracias a la novia, se fue tratado con una buena comida

En el Pozo

En un arroyo sin agua,

Hubo un pez luchando y diciendo,

"Por favor, sálvame, por favor, sálvame!"

Un ciego vio y gritó,

"Ayuda ayuda!

Hay un pez luchando aquí!"

Un sordo lo oyó y dijo,

"¿Hay alguien ahí? ¿Hay alguien ahí?

Alguien por favor venga y socorrer este pez fuera del agua!"

Un lisiado vino corriendo y dijo

Que llevaría el pez fuera del agua

Pero un monje usando un moño corrió primero

Y salvo el pez

Y mientras corría arriba y abajo

Gritando, "¡El pez está vivo ahora!"

El pez saltó al agua

La gente se reunió para examinar el pozo

Pero no había ninguno pez

Sólo mentiras flotando

Sólo mentiras flotando

Llámalo Muk de Nuevo

Durante la guerra, el rey se refugió

Y estaba comiendo una comida en la casa de un granjero

El pescado en la mesa real era tan bueno que

El rey preguntou el granjero lo que era el nombre del pescado

El granjero dijo, "El pez se llama Muk[15]."

El rey dijo, "¿Por qué ponerle el nombre de un pez tan deliciosa

como eso?"

Y dijo el granjero para llámalo Sweetfish

Después de la guerra, el rey volvió al palacio real

Y comía el pescado en la mesa real

Y dijo, "Esto sabe horrible. Esto sabe horrible.

Cómo se llama este pescado?"

---

15) Es una comida coreana hecho de almidón de cereals, judías o frutos secos, como
el alforón, el sesame y la bellota, que tiene una consistencia parecida a la de la
gelatina

El granjero dijo, "El pez se llama Sweetfish."

El rey dijo, ""¿Por qué ponerle el nombre de un pez tan horrible como eso?"

Y dijo el granjero para llámalo Muk de nuevo

Agujas de Pino

El dios del monte Paektu[16] y el dragón Rey del Mar del Este
Decidieron reunirse en calle Jongno
Para comparar y ver quién tenía más posesiones

El dios del monte Paektu dijo que
Toda la hierba y los árboles son suyo
Y el dragon Rey del Mar del Este dijo que
Todos los peces son suyo

Mientras ellos estaban contando juntos para ver quién tenía más
posesiones,
El dios del monte Paektu pensó que
Habría un menor número de hierba y los árboles
Y decidió jugar un truco

Él arrancó hojas de pino enteros
Uno a uno y rápidamente aumentó el número de hojas
Y empató con el dragón Rey del Mar del Este con dificultad

---

16) Es una montaña volcánica en la frontera entre Corea del Norte y China

Pretendiendo do Ser Mudos

Tres amigos se reunieron
Y acordaron
Para solicitar una comida
Actuando como mudos

Cuando llegó la hora del almuerzo,
Se fueron a la parte delantera de la puerta de una familia rica
Y estaban en pie en silencio
La hora del almuerzo pasó
Y todavía nadie vino a darles alimentos

Uno de los tres de ellos gritó,
"Dame un poco de comida, por favor!"
El otro le reprendió por hablar
Cuando habían acordado que fingir ser mudos

El otro amigo se jactó para los dos
Y dije, "yo soy diferente a ustedes.
Voy a ser una buen mudo
Y no voy a decir una palabra."

La Esposa de Señor Kim

Señor Kim vive con su padre Viejo

Y su esposa maltrata a su padre día y noche

Eso siempre le molestó

Entonces, el señor Kim decidió utilizar un truco y dijo a su

esposa,

"Querida, me fui al mercado y

Tu puedes vender un viejo gordo a un alto precio."

Después de escuchar eso,

La esposa pensó, 'Sería fantástico si pudiéramos engordar

El suegro y venderlo.'

Y ella fue muy amable con el suegro

El suegro estaba feliz porque

Estaba llevando bien con su nuera

Él contaba historias a sus nietos, cuidó de sus estudios

Y se fue a buscar agua para su nuera

Y lo puso en la cocina

Después había pasado mucho tiempo,

Señor Kim dijo a su esposa,

"Querida, vamos a vender a mi papá en el mercado ahora."

La esposa del señor Kim se enojó y gritó,

"De ninguna manera! Esto no va a suceder!"

El Estúpido Yerno

Érase una vez, una familia tenía un yerno

Y el suegro pensó que el yerno era muy estúpido

El suegro decidió que no podía dejar el yerno solo

Y le hizo aprender las letras

El suegro le dijo,

"Todo lo que tienes que hacer es

Copiar lo que hago.

Es un simple juego de niños.

Como yo soy el suegro, voy a empezar primero."

El yerno también copió "Voy a empezar primero."

Y cuando el suegro dijo, "Copie me sin decir la parte

'Voy a empezar primero'."

El yerno también copió "Copie me sin decir la parte

'Voy a empezar primero'."

El suegro pensó que no había esperanza de enseñarlo letras

Cuando el suegro le dijo, "Hombre, rendirse."

El yerno también copió, "Rendirse."

Él pujantemente copió el "Rendirse."

Por Qué El Agua del Mar es Salada

Érase una vez, había una muela de molino que surgió todo lo que pedimos

Cuando dices, "Salir, arroz." Y gira la muelda de molino, arroz emergería

Cuando dices, "Salir, dinero." Y gira la muelda de molino, dinero emergería

Cuando dices, "Salir, ropas." Y gira la muelda de molino, ropas emergería

Cuando dices, "Salir, sal." Y gira la muelda de molino, sal emergería

Cuando dices, "Salir, carne." Y gira la muelda de molino, carne emergería

Caundo dices, "Salir, frutas." Y gira la muelda de molino, frutas emergería

Un ladrón que de alguna manera se enteró de la muela de molino,

Se robó la muela de molino,

Cargó en su barco y estaba en camino

Cuando dijo, "salir, sal." Y giró la muelda de molino

De repente, la sal se derramaron continuamente

Y inundó el barco y no se detuvo allí

El barco se hundió en el mar con la muela de molino

Hasta hoy día, la muela de molino continúa girando, derramando sal

Y todavía no hay nadie que sabe cómo parar la muela de molino

Es por eso que el agua del mar es salada y sigue siendo salada

El Agua de la Fuente

En la dinastía Joseon, había un hombre viejo
Quien vivió cerca del Monte Kumgang[17]
Un día, él llevaba una escalerilla[18] en la espaldas
Y fue a preparar leña en las montañas
Después de cortar un montón de árboles, él tenía sed
Y bebió de la fuente
Pero el agua no era agua común
Entonces, después de que el viejo tomó un trago de agua
Se convirtió en un hombre joven de nuevo, un hombre vigoroso

Después de ver el abuelo llegó a casa como un hombre joven,
La abuela era tan celoso
Que ella siguió el abuelo para preparar leña en las montañas al
día siguiente
Y bebió el agua de la fuente aunque no tenía sed
Pero la abuela bebió demasiada agua
Que se convirtió en una bebé
Y el abuelo no la reconoció
Nunca jamás reconoció de nuevo a quien era la bebé

---

17) Es una de las montañas más conocidas de Corea del Norte
18) Portaequipajes típico coreano de la forma A

La Orina del Dios

Había una vez,

Dios descendió a la cumbre del monte Paektu

Y empezó a buscar lugares para orinar

Porque necesitaba hacer pis

Pero él simplemente no podía encontrar un lugar para orinar

Entonces, él acabó orinando

En la cima del monte Paektu

Por lo tanto, la cumbre del monte Paektu

Se cavó profundamente y se convirtió en el Lago Tianchi

Y el agua que inundó al este

Se convirtió en el río Tumen, que fluye hasta hoy día

Y el agua que inundó al oeste

Se convirtió en el río Yalu, que fluye hasta hoy día

La Chinche de Cama, la Pulga, y el Piojo

La chinche de cama, la pulga, y el piojo son hermanos

La chinche de cama, el hermano mayor

La pulga, el segundo hermano

Y el piojo, el hermano menor

La chinche de cama y la pulga

No escuchan a sus padres

Y beben día y noche

El piojo estudia mucho

Un día, la chinche de cama y la pulga bebían

Y se metió en una pelea

El piojo dijo a los hermanos,

"Hermanos, no luchan!"

Y trató de parar la pelea

Pero él fue empujado con fuerza y cayó al suelo

Y fue contusionado con una marca negra y azul en la espalda

La chinche de cama y la pulga comenzaron a sentirse mareado

Y se volvieron rojos

Así que la espalda del piojo todavía es negro y azul

La chinche de cama es de color rojo

Y la pulga es de color rojo

El Palacio Gyeongbokgung

Había un monje budista llamado Muhak,

Quién ayudó el primer rey de la dinastía Joseon, Yi Seong-Gye

Cuando Muhak estaba construyendo el palacio Gyeongbokgung,

Se dio cuenta que siguió al colapso si él construyó aquí

Luego se fue por aquí y allá

Para construir en otro lugar

Un día, se fue a un lugar

Y un granjero estaba cultivando el campo, mientras conduciendo

una vaca

Pero la vaca no escuchó al granjero

Y no cultivaba los campos bien

Entonces el granjero reprendió la vaca y dijo,

"Ugh, esta vaca! Eres estúpido como Muhak!"

Muhak, el monje budista, fingió inocencia

Y preguntó, "¿Cómo es que Muhak es estúpido?"

El granjero dijo, "El lugar llamado Hanyang[19) tiene la forma de

una garza

Entonces las cuatro puertas principales de Seúl tienen que ser

construido primero para fijar las alas de la garza

Pero Muhak no sabe cómo hacer esto, entonces no es estúpido?"

Después de escuchar el granjero, Muhak dijo,

"Es verdad.

Eso es definitivamente cierto."

Y construyó las cuatro puertas principales de Seúl primero

E después construyó el Palacio Gyeongbokgung más tarde

Después de eso, el Palacio Gyeongbokgung verdaderamente

Nunca se derrumbó de nuevo

---

19)   La capital de Joseon, corrientemente conocido como Seúl

La Corvina Amarilla

Señor Parque, un viejo avaro desde Jinju[20]
Dibujó un corvina amarilla y se colgó en el techo
Y cada vez que su familia comían la cena,
Les hizo recoger una cuchara llena de arroz,
Mirar el dibujó una vez,
Y luego comer sus comidas

Su familia dijo,
"Si te vas a hacernos comer
Con un dibujo de una corvina amarilla,
Podría haber muy bien apenas dibujado
Dos
O tres corvinas amarillas en vez."

---

20) Una ciudad ubicada en la provincial de Gyeongsang del Sur

Lo que es aún peor fue cuando

Él reprendió severamente a su familia,

"Come sólo un poco. Come sólo un poco.

Podrían tenga que beber mucha agua."

Cuando ellos accidentalmente levantaron la vista

Por sólo un poco demasiado largo

El Costo de La Torta de Arroz

Un vendedor de la torta de arroz [21)

Dejó su asiento por un segundo

Y todos los pasteles de arroz habían desaparecido

El vendedor de torta de arroz corrió al magistrado

Y le dijo que había perdido toas las tortas de arroz que estaba

vendiendo

Y le pidió que encontrarlos

El magistrado llamó a todos

Y les dio a cada uno un vaso de agua

Y les dijo, "Esta agua es medicina

Entonces no la trague

Y ponlo en tu boca

Y escupirlo de nuevo."

---

21)   Una comida tradicional Coreana

Todos hicieron lo que se les dijo

Y todos bebieron un trago de agua y escupieron la agua

Y luego, el magistrado miró a cada uno de saliva

Y uno por uno encontró a todos

Que tenía los despojos de la torta de arroz en su saliva

Y les hizo pagar el costo de las tortas de arroz

La Marica que se Convirtió Viril

Un zorro miró hacia al nido de una marica y dijo a la marica,

"Si me das uno de sus polluelos, no te mataré."

La marica tenía miedo del zorro

Y así se dio uno de sus polluelos al zorro

Después de comer un polluelo de la marica, el zorro dijo otra

vez,

"Si me das uno de sus polluelos, no te mataré."

Y así se dio otro de sus polluelos al zorro

La marica se estremeció de miedo

Una garza estaba pasando y le preguntó, "¿Qué pasó?"

La marica dijo, "Es por causa del zorro

El zorro es muy terrible que no puedo aguantarlo más."

Y luego, la garza dijo a la marica,

"El zorro no puede trepar a los árboles, entonces

Cuando el zorro viene, dile imponente,

Para tratar de subir al árbol."

El zorro se volvió y dijo a la marica,

"Si me das uno de sus polluelos, no te mataré."

Esta vez, la marica no tenía miedo del zorro y dijo imponente,

"Me atrevo a tratar de subir al árbol."

El zorro luchó para subir el árbol varias veces

Pero él sólo miró furiosamente y regresó

Él nunca subió al árbol

Y él sólo miró furiosamente y regresó

El Dueño Malicioso y el Hijo del Sirviente

Érase una vez,

Un dueño malicioso

Le dijo a su sirviente de su casa

Para ir a las montañas

Y recoger frambuesas

A pesar de que era un invierno muy frío

Después de escuchar el dueño,

El sirviente no sabía qué hacer

Entonces su hijo fue a el dueño y le preguntó,

"Mi padre fue a recoger frambuesas en las montañas

Y fue mordido por una serpiente. Eso es terrible!

¿Qué medicamentos debo usar?"

El dueño dijo,

"No hay serpientes en este invierno frío."

El hijo del sirviente replicó y dijo,

"No hay frambuesas en este invierno frío también!"

El dueño se apercibió y dijo,

"Vamos fingir que nunca le dije a nadie para ir a recoger frambuesas."

El Plenilunio

Érase una vez, en una pequeña ciudad,

Hubo un magistrado estúpido

Era el último día del mes, así que no había la luna en el cielo

El magistrado estúpido se preocupó y llamó al administrador

El administrador le dijo al magistrado estúpido,

"La luna fue comprado con dinero y colgó sobre el cielo

Para que la gente de la pequeña ciudad

puedan pasar en la noche también.

Un magistrado compró y lo colgó sobre el cielo."

El magistrado estúpido preguntó al administrador

Cuanto tiene que pagar para comprar la luna

El administrador le dijo al magistrado estúpido,

"Sólo tienes que pagar 2000 Ñang[22] para comprar a la luna."

---

22) Unidad de la moneda anitgua coreana

En la noche siguiente, el administrador dijo el magistrado,

"¡Mira! Compré la luna y colgué encima del cielo."

El magistrado estúpido levantó la vista al cielo

Y vio la luna nueva colgado

Él dijo que la luna era demasiado pequeño e inútil

El administrador le dijo al magistrado estúpido que era porque

El precio de la luna subió mucho

El magistrado dijo que el administrador debe comprar la luna

grande

A pesar de que cuesta un montón de dinero

Unos días más tarde,

El administrador compró la luna grande, con diez mil Ñang

Y lo colgó sombre el cielo

Y dijo al magistrado estúpido para mirar el cielo

El plenilunio estaba colgado sobre el cielo

La Primera Vez Señor Lee Fue Engañado

Señor Lee simpre se jactó que

Nunca había sido engañado por nadie toda su vida

Un día de invierno muy frío, un amigo vino a visitarlo

Y el amigo dijo, "Yo vi una cereza del tamaño de una sandía

En un cerezo en mi camino aquí."

Despúes de escuchar eso, Lee dijo,

"No hay tal cosa como una cereza del tamaño de una sandía.

No voy a ser engañado por eso. ¡Nunca voy a ser engañado por

eso!"

Pero el amigo dijo,

¡Ví con mis propios ojos!

Yo hasta ví una cereza del tamaño de un melón."

Despúes de escuchar eso, Lee dijo,

"No hay tal cosa como una cereza del tamaño de un melón.

No voy a ser engañado por eso. ¡Nunca voy a ser engañado por

eso!"

Sería creíble si era

El tamaño de un durazno o una ciruela."

Y luego, el amigo dijo,

"Realmente nunca ha estado engañado por nadie antes?

Entonces yo te engañé por primera vez.

¿Cómo sería una cereza crecer en este invierno muy frío?

Jajaja!"

Y rió a carcajadas. Él se rió abiertamente.

Monte Paektu y el Monte Halla

Mucho, mucho, mucho tiempo atrás

Abuelo Paektu

Comió azufaifas

Y siempre tiró las semillas

Para un lugar

Las semillas apilaron y apilaron

Y se convirtió en una montaña

Desde entonces,

Las personas nombraron la montaña después del abuelo

Y lo llamaron Monte Paektu

Mucho, mucho, mucho tiempo atrás

Abuelo Halla

Siempre tiró piedras de Baduc[23]

Para un lugar

Cada vez que la tierra y el mar se invirtieron

---

23) Un juego coreano de fichas blancas y negras

Las semillas apilaron y apilaron

Y se convirtió en una montaña

Desde entonces,

Las personas nombraron la montaña después del abuelo

Y lo llamaron Monte Halla

Jactando Sus Edades

Érase una vez,

El tigre, el zorro y el sapo

Cada argumentaron que

Ellos eran mayores que el otro

El tigre dijo primero, "Yo nací en los tiempos antiguos

Del emperador japonés."

Después, el zorro dijo, "Yo nací durante

El gobierno de Shennong[24]."

Pero el sapo no dijo nada

Y derramó lágrimas gruesas

El tigre y el zorro

Dijeron al sapo,

"¿Entonces, estás llorando porque

Naciste última, verdad?"

---

24) Shennong, también es conocido como Emperador Yan, es uno de los personajes
principales de la mitología China

Pero el sapo les dijo,

"Eso absolutamente no es la razón.

Estoy llorando porque

Me acordé de repente

Mi hijo mayor

Quien nació en los tiempos antiguos

Del emperador japonés

Y mi segundo hijo

Que nació en

El gobierno de Shennong

Después de escuchar el sapo,

El tigre y el zorro estaban vergonzosos

Por jactar sus edades

Delante del sapo

Y le rogaron el perdón y dijeron,

"Abuelo sapo,

Por favor, perdónanos,

Por favor perdónanos."

El Sirviente del Oficial Señor Kim de Andong

Oficial Señor Kim, que vivía en Andong,

Iba a Seúl con su sirviente

Él tenía mucho hambre

Y dijo a su sirviente para ir comprarlo

Un tazón de sopa

El sirviente compró un tazón de sopa

Pero siguió recogiendo sus bolsillos

En su camino de vuelta

Cuando Oficial Señor Kim le preguntó

Lo que estaba buscando en sus bolsillos,

El sirviente le respondió,

"Se me cayó una legaña en la sopa

En mi camino aquí

Y yo estaba buscando lo

Pero el aceite se ve como la legaña

Y la legaña parece demasiado al aceite

Por lo tanto, es imposible encontrarlo.

Eso es terrible!"

Después de escuchar eso, el oficial Señor Kim

Perdió su apetito

Y dijo al sirviente

Para tirar la sopa

O comer lo

O hacer lo que quiera

Después de escuchar eso, el sirviente pensó,

'¡Sí! ¡Hurra!'

Y se comió el tazón de sopa en un instante

Yo También Soy Un Castaño

El profesor Lee Yulgok de la Dinastía Joseon
Estaba destinado a ser mordido por un tigre
Alguien dijo una vez, "Si plantas mil
Castaños, no será mordido por un tigre."
Entonces, su familia habían plantado mil castaños

Pero un día, mientras que Lee Yulgok estaba jugando solo en
casa,
Un tigre se acercó y dijo, "Vamos a contar juntos cuántos
Castaños están planteados en su casa!"

Un árbol, dos árboles, tres árboles
Ellos contaron los árboles juntos
Cuando algo grande sucedió
Sólo había 999 castaños
Había exactamente un árbol
Faltando de los 1000 árboles

El tigre abrió su boca y dijo,

"Dado que hay un árbol faltando

De los árboles plantados aquí,

¡Te voy a comer!"

Y atacó el profesor Lee Yulgok

Pero en ese momento, el profesor Lee Yulgok agitó las manos y
le dijo,

"¡Mira! Yo también soy un castaño! También soy un castaño!

Después de escuchar eso, el tigre dijo,

"Ah bien! Entonces está exactamente un mil árboles! Hay 1,000
árboles!"

Y se volvió a las montañas

El Hombre Que Fue Elegido Como el Administrador

Hace mucho tiempo, en un pueblo en Daegu,

El nuevo magistrado de Seúl vino

Y cuatro personas se ofrecieron para ser el administrador

El nuevo magistrado contemplaba a quien

Se debe elegir como su administrador

Él decidió que iba a elegir la persona que

Pudiera adivinar su pregunta difícil

Como su administrador

El nuevo magistrado contempló y contempló

Y hizo una pregunta,

"¿Cuántas montañas hay en Daegu?"

Señor Lee respondió, "Eso es más de lo que puedo responder

Porque hay más de uno o dos montañas aquí."

Señor Kim dijo, "Hay la montaña Palgong, la montaña Biseul,

Y la montaña Duryu."

Señor Parque dijo, "Hay una gran montaña

y una pequeña montaña."

Y, por último, el Señor Hong dijo, "Hay

Un total de cuatro montañas en Daegu.

En la primavera, hay la montaña de la flor,

En el verano, hay la montaña verde,

En el otoño, hay la montaña de hojas amarillas

En el invierno, hay la montaña blanca."

Después de escuchar al Señor Hong, al nuevo magistrado pensó,

"Si, eso es!" Y eligió al Señor Hong como su administrador

Vamos A Sólo Comer Torta de Arroz

Un millonario frugal que no no tenía ni idea
De como hacer una torta de arroz
Tenía una nuera
Un día, la nuera preguntó
Por qué él nunca hizo una torta de arroz
El millonario simplemente respondió,
"Es sólo una pérdida para hacer una torta de arroz."

Después de escuchar el millonario,
La nuera bañó tres doe[25)] de arroz en el agua
Delante del millonario
Y aventó el arroz para que parecía que
Había seis doe de arroz
Y mostró el millonario nuevo

---

25) Una medida coreana de capacidad

Después de mirarlo, el millonario frugal dijo,

"Supongo que no es una pérdida

Para hacer una torta de arroz.

Mi querida, vamos a hacer una torta de arroz.

Vamos a hacer una torta de arroz."

La nuera hizo una torta de arroz adicionando

Frijol puré y dio la torta a millonario frugal

El millonario frugal comió la torta y le dijo,

"No vamos a comer arroz más.

Querida, vamos a sólo comer torta de arroz.

Vamos a sólo comer torta de arroz.

Es tan delicioso y además,

No hay ninguna pérdida haciendo la torta.

Vamos a sólo comer torta de arroz."

La Nuera Muda

Hace mucho tiempo, cuando una señorita

Se iba a casar, su padre le amonestó

Diciendo, "Querida, cuando estas casado,

Vive 9 años así: Tres años como una muda,

Tres años como una persona sorda,

Y tres años como una persona ciega."

La señorita nunca habló después de que ella se casó

Ella sólo habló en gestos

El suegro no podía aguantar a ella más

Y llamó sus sirvientes

Y les dijo que la llevará de vuelta a sus padres

Los sirvientes llevaron a señorita

En una litera de nuevo a sus padres

Pero cuando ellos pasaron por un pinar

Ellos la dejaron salir de la litera

Así que ella podía hacer pis

Ella vio un faisán sentado en el pinar

Y dijo, "Me gustaría poder coger ese faisán

Y hacer un plato de acompañamiento

Y servir a mi suegro."

Después de escuchar eso, los sirvientes le pusieron en la litera de

nuevo

Y se la llevó de vuelta a su suegro

Y ellos le dijeron que ella había hablado

El suegro estaba muy contento y comenzó a bailar

Bailó con gran alegría

El Conejo

Un cazador fue a cazar y vio un conejo
Y disparó la pierna de conejo con un arma
El conejo se lanzó con una cojera

Un perro estaba caminando por el camino de una montaña
Cuando vio al conejo corriendo con una cojera
Él corrió hacia el conejo y le mordió
Y se llevó a su casa

El cazador siguió al perro jadeando
Sólo había un niño de siete años
Dentro de la casa

El cazador le dijo a devolver a su conejo
Y la niña dijo escrupulosamente,
"El que hizo la pierna del conejo cojera es a ti
Pero sin duda fue mi perro que atrapó al conejo

Y ya que necesitas la piel de conejo y

Mi perro necesita carne

Tu puedes tener la piel de conejo y

Vamos a dar a mi perro la carne de conejo."

La Gente Que Eran Parcialmente Sordas

Hace mucho tiempo, en una casa en el distrito de Gyeongsang

Allí vivía una una nuera parcialmente sorda,

Una suegra parcialmente sorda, y un sirviente parcialmente sordo

Un día, la nuera estaba en la cocina

Y dijo que iba a hacer el desayuno

Y comenzó a preparar platos de acompañamiento

Mientras golpeando el tajo de cocina

La suegra ni siquiera oyó el ruido claramente

Y dijo desde el dormitorio,

"Querida, ¿qué estás diciendo?

No echa la culpa a mí!"

La nuera ni siquiera oyó la suerga claramente

Y dijo desde la cocina,

"Me estás regañando de nuevo hoy

Por algo que ocurrió hace tres días!'

El sirviente ni siquiera oyó la nuera claramente

Y dijo desde el patio,

"Todavía me estás regañando

Por quebrar la bacinilla accidentalmente hace dos meses!"

El Profesor de la Escuel a del Pueblo

El profesor de la escuela del pueblo estaba enseñando

Una cartilla de los caracteres chinos

Pero no importa lo mucho que le enseña al estudiante estúpido,

El estudiante no entendía

Entonces el profesor dijo calmadamente para el estudiante,

"Creo que sería mejor para ti para vender pescado en vez de

estudiar.

Ir a los lugares grandes con muchas personas y decir, '¡compra

pescado!'"

El estudiante estúpido lo que le dijo a

Y fue un lugar grande con un montón de gente y dijo, "¡Compra

pescado!"

Pero este lugar era una reunión para lamentar a pérdida de un

hombre viejo

La gente se enojó y le regañó

"¡Dónde crees que estás vendiendo pescado!"

El estudiante estúpido fue a su profesor y le dijo,

"Yo sólo hice lo que dijo y fue reprendido."

Después de escuchar el estudiante, el profesor

Acarició el estudiante en sus hombros y con calma le dijo de

nuevo

"Cuando vas a lugares como ese,

Tienes que pedir la gente primero,

'¿Estás bien?'"

El estudiante estúpido dijo, "Muy bien, Señor." Y fue

Para un lugar grande con un montón de gente y preguntó las

personas,

"¿Estás bien?"

Pero era una reunión para celebrar el 70 aniversario de un

hombre viejo

 La gente se enojó y le regañó

"¡Dónde crees que estás preguntando a la gente si están bien!"

El Hijo del Multimillonario e la Hija del Millonario

Un día, el multimillonario

Preguntó a su nuera

Que era la hija del millonario

"¿Sabes cómo poner la mesa?"

"No lo sé, señor."

"¿Sabes cómo tejer la tela?"

"No lo sé, señor."

"¿Sabes cómo coser prendas?"

"No lo sé, señor."

Cada vez que alguien preguntó algo,

Ella siempre decía,

"No lo sé, no lo sé."

Un día, el millonario

Preguntó a su yerno

Que era el hijo del multimillonario

"¿Sabes cómo recoger leñas?"

Él inmediatamente fue a las montañas

Y volvió con un montón de árboles

"¿Sabes cómo hacer sandalias de paja?"

Él inmediatamente hizo un par de sandalias

"¿Sabes cómo cortar madera?"

Él inmediatamente cortó un montón de leña

No había trabajo que él no podía hacer

No había nada que no podía hacer

Las Cigarras del Monte Seorak

Hace mucho mucho tiempo, no había cigarras

En Monte Seorak

¿Cómo es que hay tantas cigarras ahora?

Es porque todos vinieron de Ulsan

Había un taoísta viviendo en Ulsan

Y todo lo que hizo durante todo el día

Era comer y dormir

Un verano, las cigarras

Estaban llorando demasiado alto

Que el taoísta no podía dormir

Así que decidió hacer las cigarras callar

Y trató de maldecirlos y soplar todas las cigarras

Pero las cigarras eran muy astutos

Y sintieron lo que el taoísta iba a hacer

Y volaron todo el camino hasta el monte Seorak

Para evitar la maldición

Y desde entonces,

Había cigarras viviendo en el Monte Seorak también

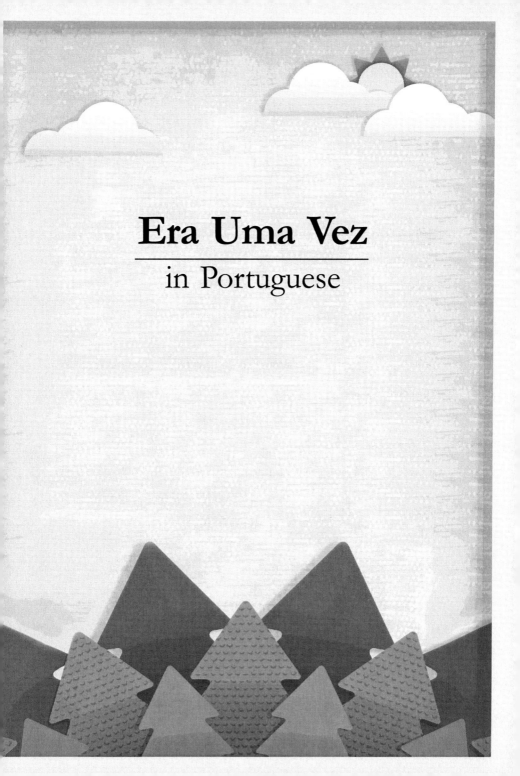

Era Uma Vez

in Portuguese

O Malandro que Impressionou o Tigre

Havia um malandro
Que não ir ao banheiro quando tinha que fazer xixi no meio da
noite
Mas ao invés, ele foi para ir fazer xixi na cozinha
O deus da cozinha
Não podia aguentar o cheiro de urina mais
E pediu o deus da montanha para repreender o diabinho

O deus da montanha, que tinha recebido o favor do deus da
cozinha
Chamou o tigre que é bom em fazer recados
E ele lhe disse isso,
"Se você ir para o centro, há um malandro que faz xixi na
cozinha.
Vá ali e repreendê-lo severamente por mim!"

O tigre veio até a aldeia
E se escondeu atrás do quintal do malandro
Ele se escondeu lá, permanecendo sem mover

No meio da noite,

O malandro realmente entrou na cozinha

E fez xixi balbuciante

O tigre levantou-se para repreender o menino travesso

Mas o menino começou a murmurar para si mesmo

O tigre animou seus ouvidos para ouvir o menino e ouviou-o

dizer,

"Se eu estou congelando até mesmo quando eu estou confinado

em casa,

O tigre deve ser muito frio!"

Depois de ouvir o malandro falar,

O tigre decidiu que não poderia repreender

Um menino que amava ele tanto

E ele voltou para as montanhas

E decidiu que seria melhor para ele ser repreendido pelo o deus

da montanha

E voltou para as montanhas

O Bezerro que Foi Dividido em Dois

Em uma aldeia chamada Gyeongju no distrito de Gyeonsang,
Um fazendeiro estava alimentando uma vaca de otra pessoa
Ela estava gravida e por isso tinha uma barriga saliente
A vaca finalmente pariu
E deu à luz a dois bezerros ao mesmo tempo

O fazendeiro queria um
Dos dois bezerros para si mesmo
Então, ele foi para a aldeia vizinha
Para encontrar o dono da vaca
E não contei a ele que o vaca deu à luz a dois bezerros
Mas disse que havia somente um bezerro

Depois de ouvir o fazendeiro, o dono da vaca disse,
"Você poderia ter apenas disse que a vaca deu à luz a bezerro
em vez de um bezerro.
Isso é muito estranho, Isso e muito estranho.
Eles disseram que minha vaca

Sempre daria à luz a dois bezerros ao mesmo tempo."

E depois, o fazendeiro disse honestamente,

"Eu acho que há uma otra vaca que

Dá à luz a dois bezerros ao mesmo tempo."

Depois, o dono da vaca sorriu e disse,

"Dar à luz a dois bezerros significa para compartilhar os bezerros."

E ele deu um bezerro para o fazendeiro

A Mosca Mais Desagradável do Mundo

Um velho avarento chamada Jung, que mora no Chungju,
Estava almoçando no campo
Com apenas um pequeno prato de molho de soja
E um tigela de cevada cozida depois de fazer
O trabalho agrícola em um dia quente de verão

Mas enquanto comia uma colher de cevada cozida,
E estava prestes a mergulhar no molho de soja
Uma mosca desceu e sentou-se no pequeno prato de molho de
soja
E molhou sua perna no molho de soja
E rapidamente fugiu

O velho avarento Jung
Seguiu a mosca,
Dizendo que ele iria encontrar o seu precioso molho de soja
novamente
E depois de corer 500m até a Mungyeong Saejae Pass,

Ele finalmente capturou a mosca

E depois,

Detonou a mosca dizendo,

"Sua mosca desagradável!"

E chupou o molho de soja da perna da mosca

E depois, soltou a mosca

O mosquito e o Sapo

Era uma vez, havia um mosquito e um sapo

Que vivia no distrito rural

Eles decidiram fazer uma competição

Para ver quem consequia chegar

A Namdaemun[26] em Seul primeiro

O mosquito pensou secretamente,

'Não há nenhum ponto em competir

porque eu obviamente vai ganhar de qualquer jeito,

como eu obviamente posso voar e

o sapo vai ter que engatinhar todo o caminho até lá.'

Mas depois de realmente fazê-lo,

Não foi tão fácil como o mosquito tinha pensado

Com chuva ou com sol,

O sapo lentamente se engatinhou para frente

---

26)   O Grande Portão Sul de Seul

Mas depois de realmente competir,

Não foi tão fácil como ele tinha pensado

Quando era ventoso ou chovendo

O mosquito não podia voar

E por causa disso,

O sapo chegou a Namdaemun primeiro

E quando o mosquito chegou alguns dias mais tarde,

O sapo colocou uma atitude arrogante, vangloriou-se, e disse,

"Ahem, ahem. Olha.

As sandálias de palha eu estou sentado no completamente

estragou."

O Touro Grávida

Dolse, o filho de sete anos do Senhor Kim,
Foi à procurar a vossa excelência, senhor Hong
E preguntou ao ele, "Senhor, senhor.
Meu pai deu à luz um bebê saudável hoje
E a gente não temos alga marinha em nossa casa.
Você poderia dar-nos um pouco de alga marinha?

Depois de ouvir isso, Senhor Hong riu em voz alta e disse,
"Ai, pequenininho. Como pode um homem dar à luz a uma
criança?"
Mas o menino não deu e disse,
"Senhor, senhor. Cadê o touro grávida?"

E depois, senhor Hong se lembrava recentemente dizendo
Para o Senhor Kim que ele seria repreendido
Se ele não trouxe Hong o touro grávida
E sentindo-se vergonhosa, disse,
"Eu sinto muito,
sinto muito."
Para o menino

Porque o Sapo tem Uma Barriga Arredondada

Um dia, a raposa, o coelho, e o sapo
Fizeram um bolo de arroz e decidiram que
A pessoa que é pior em bebendo alcool
Teria que comer todo o bolo de arroz

O coelho foi o primeiro a aceitar alegremente
E disse, "Eu fico bêbada somente por indo perto de um campo de
trigo."
A raposa disse, "Eu fico bêbada só de olhar para o rosto do
coelho bêbado."

O sapo não disse nada
Quando o coelho e a raposa preguntaram
por que ele não estava dizendo nenhuma palavra,
O sapo disse, "Eu já estou bêbado somente ouvindo vocês
que eu não posso falar."

E disse que a pessoa que é pior em bebendo alcool é ele
E ele comeu todo o bolo de arroz
E é por isso
Que o sapo tem uma barriga arredondada

O Noivo Travesso

Na dinastia Joseon,

Senhor Song Si-Yeol era um famoso espertalhão quando era
jovem

Na cerimônia de casamento, a noiva não tem permissão para
falar

Mas quando seus amigos lhe pediu para fazer uma aposta,

Para ver se ele poderia fazer a noiva falar no casamento,

O noivo estava cheio de confiança

Então, no dia em que o noivo ia se casar, ele entrou o casamento

E era a sua vez de saudar-se à noiva

Mas ele não saudou de propósito e só ficou de pé

"Saudar-se a ela. Rapidamente, rapidamente." Pessoas lhe disse

Mas ele só ficou de pé rigidamente

Quando as pessoas preguntavam por que ele estava parado

Ele disse, "Minha avó é um muda

Minha mãe é um muda

E se minha noiva também é um muda, eu nunca vou me casar."

E disse a noiva para falar alguma coisa

A noiva não tinha permissão de falar no casamento

Mas ela só tinha que depois de ouvir o que o noivo disse

E porque a noiva falou na cerimônia de casamento,

O noivo Song Si-Yeol ganhou a aposta com seus amigos

E graças a noiva, foi tratada com uma refeição agradável de seus amigos

Dentro do Poço

Em um córrego sem água,
Havia um peixe se debatendo e dizendo,
"Por favor me salve, por favor me salve!"

Uma pessoa cega viu e gritou,
"Socorro, Socorro!
Há um peixe debatendo aqui!"

Uma pessoa surda ouviu isso e disse,
"Alguém aí? Alguém aí?
Alguém por favor venha e tirar este peixe fora da água!"

Uma pessoa aleijado veio correndo e disse
Que iria tirar a peixe fora da água
Mais um monge vestindo um topete veio correndo primeiro
E salvou o peixe

E enquanto correndo para cima e para baixo

Gritando, "O peixe está vivo agora!"

O peixe pulou na água

Pessoas se reuniram para olhar dentro do poço

Mas não havia nenhum peixe

Só havia mentiras flutuando ao redor

Só mentiras flutuando ao redor

Chamá-lo Muk de Novo

Durante a guerra, o rei refugiou-se
E estava comendo uma refeição na casa de um fazendeiro
O peixe na mesa real era tão bom que
O rei preguntou ao fazendeiro o que o nome do peixe era

O fazendeiro disse, "O peixe é chamado Muk[27]."
O rei disse, "Por que você iria nomeá-lo um peixe tão delicioso assim?"
E disse ao fazendeiro para chamá-lo Sweetfish

Depois da guerra, o rei voltou para o palácio real
E comeu o peixe na mesa real
E falou, "Este gosto horrível. Este gosto horrível.
Como se chama esse peixe?"

---

27) É uma comida coreana feita a partir de grãos, feijões, ou amido de porca, tal como trigo, gergelim, e bolota e tem uma consistência gelatinosa

O fazendeiro disse, "O peixe é chamado Sweetfish."

O rei disse, "Por que você iria nomeá-lo um peixe tão horrível assim?"

E disse ao fazendeiro para chamá-lo Muk de novo

Agulhas de Pinheiro

O deus do montanha Baekdu[28] e o deus dragão do mar do leste
Dediciram reunir-se mutuamente em Rua Jongno
Para comparar e veja quem tinha mais haveres

O deus do montanha Baekdu disse que
Toda a grama e as árvores são seu
E o deuse dragão do mar do leste disse que
Todos os peixes são seu

Enquanto eles estavam contando juntos para ver quem tinha mais
haveres,
O deuse do montanha baekdu pensou que
Haveria um menor número de grama e árvores
E decidiu jogar uma manha

---

28) Uma montanha vulcânica localizada na fronteira da Coreia da Norte com a China

Ele arrancou agulhas de pinheiro inteiras

Um por um e rapidamente aumentou o número de folhas

E empatou dificilmente com o deus dragão do mar do leste

Fingindo de Ser Mudos

Três amigos reuniram

E concordaram

Em pedir pelo uma refeição

Agindo como mudos

Quando chegou a hora de almoço,

Eles foram para a frente do portão de uma família rica

E ficaram de pé silenciosamente

A hora de almoço passou

E ainda ninguém veio para dar-lhes comida

Um dos três deles gritou,

"Me dar um pouco de comida, por favor!"

O outro repreendeu a ele por falar

Quando eles haviam concordado para fingir ser mudos

O outro amigo se-vangloriou para os dois

E disse, "Eu sou diferente de vocês.

Eu vou ser um bom mudo

E não vou dizer nenhuma palavra."

A Esposa do Senhor Kim

Senhor Kim vive com seu pai velho

E sua esposa maltrata seu pai dia e noite

Isso sempre pesou em seu consciência

Então Senhor Kim decidiu jogar uma manha

E disse para sua esposa,

"Querida, eu fui para o mercado e

você pode vender um velho gordo a um preço elevado."

Depois de ouvir isso,

 A esposa pensou, 'Seria ótimo se pudéssemos engordar

O sôgro

E vendê-lo.'

E ela foi muito amável com o sôgro

O sôgro estava muito feliz porque ele estava

Se dando bem com sua nora.

Ele contou histórias para seus netos, cuidou de seus estudos

E até foi buscar água para a nora

E colocá-lo na cozinha

Depois de muito tempo se passou,

Senhor Kim disse a esposa,

"Querida, vamos vendê meu pai no mercado agora."

A esposa de Senhor kim ficou raivosa e gritou,

"De jeito nenhum! Isso não vai acontecer!"

O Estúpido Genro

Era uma vez, uma família tinham um genro
E o sôgro penseou que ele era estúpido
O sôgro decidiu que não podia deixar o genro sozinho
E fez o genro aprender letras

O sôgro disse a ele,
"Tudo que você tem que fazer é
Copiar o que eu faço.
É um mero jogo de criança.

Como eu sou o sôgro, eu vou começar primeiro."
O genro tambem copiou "Eu vou começar primeiro."
E quando o sôgro disse, "Copiar-me sem dizer o parte
'Eu vou começar primeiro'."
O genro tambem copiou "Copiar-me sem dizer o parte
'Eu vou começar primeiro'."

O sôgro pensou que não havia esperança em ensinar-lhe letras

Quando o sôgro disse, "Cara, desiste completamente."

O genro tambem copiou "Desiste completamente."

Ele valentemente copiou o "Desiste completamente."

Por Que a Água do Mar É Salgada

Era uma vez, houve uma pedra de moer que emergiu tudo o que pedimos

Quando você diz, "Sair, arroz." e gira a pedra de moer, arroz iria emergir

Quando você diz, "Sair, dinheiro." e gira a pedra de moer, dinheiro iria emergir

Quando você diz, "Sair, ropas."e gira a pedra de moer, ropas iria emergir

Quando você diz, "Sair, sal." e gira a pedra de moer, sal iria emergir

Quando você diz, "Sair, carne." e gira a pedra de moer, carne iria emergir

Quando você diz, "Sair, frutas." e gira a pedra de moer, frutas iria emergir

Um ladrão que de algum modo encontrou sobre a pedra de moer,

Roubou a pedra,

Carregou a pedra em seu barco e estava a camino

Quando ele disse, "Sair, sal" e girou a pedra de moer

De repente, sal jorrou continuamente

E inundou o barco e não parou por aí

O barco afundou no mar com a pedra de moer

Até hoje, a pedra de moer continua a girar, jorrando sal

E ainda não há uma pessoa que sabe como parar a pedra de moer

Isso é porque a água do mar é salgado e continua a ser salgado

A Água de Fonte

Durante a dinastia Joseon, havia um homem velho
Que Morava perto do Monte Kŭmgang[29]
Um dia, ele carregava um quadro em forma de A[30] nas suas
costas
E foi para juntar lenha nas montanhas
Depois de cortar uma carga de árvores, ele ficou com sede
E bebeu da fonte
Mas a água não era água ordinária
Então, depois que o velho tomou um gole de agua,
Ele tornou-se um jovem de novo, um homem vigoroso

Depois de ver o vovô voltar para casa como um homem jovem,
A avó era tão ciumento que ela segiu a ele para junta lenha no
dia seguinte
E bebeu a água de fonte primeiro, mesmo que ela não estava
com sede
Mas a avó bebeu demasiado água
Que ela se tornou uma bebê
E o vovô não reconhecê-la
Ele nunca jamais reconheceu novamente quem a bebê era

---

29) É uma da montanhas mais famosas localizada na costa leste da Coreia do Norte
30) Um armação coreana

O Xixi de Deus

Era uma vez,

Deus desceu para o topo da montanha Baekdu

E comecou a procurar lugares para fazer xixi

Porque ele precisava fazer xixi

Mas ele simplesmente não conseguia encontrar um lugar para

fazer xixi

Então, ele acabou fazendo xixi

No topo da montanha Baekdu

Deste modo, o topo da montanha Baekdu

Foi escavado profundamente e tornou-se o lago Tianchi

E a água que inundou a leste

Tornou-se o Río Tumen, que corre até hoje

E a água que inundou a oeste

Tornou-se o Río Yalu, que corre até hoje

O Percevejo de Cama, a Pulga, e o Piolho

O percevejo de cama, a pulga, e o piolho são irmãos

O precevejo de cama, o irmão mais velho

A pulga, o segundo irmão

E o piolho, o irmão mais novo

O percevejo de cama e a pulga

Não escutam seus pais

E bebem dia e noite

O piolho estuda muito

Um dia, o percevejo de cama e a pulga beberam

E entrou em uma briga

O piolho disse aos irmãos

"Irmãos, pare de brigar!"

E tentou parar a briga

Mas ele foi empurrado forte e caiu no chão

E estava machucado com uma marca preta e azul nas suas costas

O percevejo de cama e a pulga começaram a sentir-se tonto

E ficaram vermelhos

Então, as costas do piolho ainda é preta e azul

O percevejo de cama é vermelho

E a pulga é vermelho

O Palácio Gyeongbokgung

Havia um monge budista chamado Muhak,

Quem ajudou o primeiro rei da dinastia Joseon, Yi Seong-Gye

Quando Muhak estava construindo o palácio,

Ele notou que continuou a colapsar se ele construiu aqui

Então ele passou por aqui e ali

Para construí-lo em outro lugar

Um dia, ele foi para um lugar

E um fazendeiro estava arando os campos, enquanto dirigindo

um bezerro

Mas o bezerro não escutou o fazendeiro

E não arou os campos bem

Então o faznedeiro reprendeeu o bezerro e disse,

"Ugh esse bezerro! Você é estúpido como o Muhak!"

Muhak, o monge budhista fingiu inocência

E preguntou, " Como é que o Muhak é estúpido?"

O fazendeiro disse, "O lugar chamado Hanyang[31] tem a forma

de uma garça

Então os quatro portões principais de Seul têm que ser

construídas primeiro

Para fixar as asas da garça

Mas o Muhak não sabe como fazer isso, então ele não é

estúpido?"

Depois de ouvir o faznedeiro, Muhak disse,

"Isso é verdade,

Isso é definitivamente verdadeiro."

E construiu os quarto portões principais de Seul primeiro

E depois construiu o Palácio Gyeongbokgung mais tarde

Depois disso, Palácio Gyeongbokgung verdadeiramente

Nunca entrou em um colapso novamente

---

31)   A capital do Joseon, atualmente conhecida como Seul

A Corvina Amarela

Senhor Parque, um velho avarento do Jinju[32]
Desenhou uma corvine amarela e pendurou no teto
E cada vez que sua família comeu o jantar,
Ele fez-lhes colher uma colher cheia de arroz,
Olhar para o desenho uma vez,
E depois comer a suas refeições

Sua família disse,
"Se você vai fazer a gente comer
Com um desenho de uma corvina amarela,
Você poderia ter muito bem apenas desenhada
Dois
Ou três corvinas amarelas em vez."

---

32) Uma cidade localizada na provincia de Gyeongsang de sul

O que foi ainda pior foi quando

Ele repreendeu severamente a sua família

"Come só um pouco. Come só um pouco.

Vocês podem ter que beber muita água."

Quando eles acidentalmente olharam para cima

Para o desenho para um pouco longo

O Custo do Bolo de Arroz

Um mercador de bolo de arroz[33] estava vendendo bolos de arroz

Ele saiu por um segundo

E todos os bolos de arroz desapareceram

O mercador de bolo de arroz correu para o magistrado

E disse que ele tinha perdido todos os bolos de arroz que ele

estava vendendo

E pediu-lhe para encontrá-los

O magistrado chamou a todos

E deu a cada um um copo de água

E disse-lhes, "Esta água é medicina

Então não engoli-lo

E colocá-lo em sua boca

E cuspi-lo novamente."

---

33) Uma comida tradicional de corea

Todos fizeram como que lhes mandavam

E todos tomaram um gole de água e cuspiram a água

E depois, o magistrado olhou para cada saliva

E um por um encontrou a todos

Que tinham os pedaços de bolos de arroz em sua saliva

E fez-lhes pagar o custo dos bolos de arroz

A Pêga Que se Tornou Viril

Uma raposa olhou para cima para o ninho de um pêga e disse
para o pêga,
"Se você me dar um de seus pintinhos, eu não vou te matar."
A pêga estava com medo da raposa
E então ela deu um de seus pintinhos para a raposa

Depois de comer um pintinho da pêga, a raposa novamente disse,
"Se você me dar um de seus pintinhos, eu não vou te matar."
A pêga estava com medo da raposa
E então ela deu outro de seus pintinhos para a raposa

A pêga estremeceu de medo
Um grou estava passando e preguntou, "Que passou?"
A pêga disse, "É por causa da raposa
A raposa é muito assustador que eu não posso aguentar mais. "

Aí o grou disse para a pêga,
"A raposa não pode subir em árvores, então
Quando a raposa vem, diga-lhe imponentemente,

Para tentar subir na árvore."

A raposa voltou e disse para a pêga,

"Se você me dar um de seus pintinhos, eu não vou te matar."

Desta vez, a pêga não estava com medo da raposa e disse

imponentemente,

"Eu te desafio a tentar subir a árvore."

A raposa lutava para subir na árvore várias vezes

Mas ele só olhou penetrante e ferozmente e retornou

Ele nunca subiu na árvore

E ele só olhou penetrante e ferozmente e retornou

O Dono Malicioso e o Filho do Servente

Era uma vez,

Um dono malicioso

Disse à seu servente da sua casa

Para ir para as montanhas

E colher framboesas

Apesar que era um inverno muito frio

Depois de ouvir o dono,

O servente não sabia o que fazer

Então seu filho foi para o dono e preguntou,

"Meu pai foi para colher framboesas nas montanhas

E foi mordido por uma cobra. Isso é terrível!

Qual medicina eu uso?"

O dono disse,

"Não há nenhuma cobra no inverno frio."

O filho do servente falou de volta e disse,

"Não há framboesas nesse inverno frio também!"

O dono leu a mente dele e disse,

"Vamos fingir que eu nunca disse a alguém para ir colher framboesas."

O Plenilúnio

Era uma vez. em uma pequena cidade,

Houve um magistrado estúpido

Era o último dia do mês, e por isso não havia lua no céu

O magistrado estúpido ficou preocupado e chamou o

administrador

O administrador disse ao magistrado estúpido,

"A lua foi comprado com dinheiro e pendurado acima do céu

Para que as pessoas da pequena cidade

Poderia passear durante a noite também.

Um magistrado comprou e pendurou-a acima do céu."

O magistrado estúpido preguntou ao administrador

Quanto ele tinha que pagar para comprar a lua

O administrador disse ao magistrado estúpido,

"Você só tem que pagar 2000 Nyang[34] para compar a lua."

---

34) Uma unidade antiga de cunhagem de moeda coreana

Na noite seguinte, o administrador disse ao magistrado,

"Olha! Eu comprei a lua e endurou-a acima do céu."

O magistrado estúpido olhou para o céu

E viu a lua nova pendurando

Ele disse que a lua era muita pequena e inútil

O administrador disse ao magistrado estúpido que era porque

O preço da lua levantou-se um monte

O magistrado disse ao administrador que ele deveria comprar a

lua grande

Mesmo que custa um monte de dinheiro

Alguns dias depois,

O administrador comprou a lua grande com dez mil Nyang

E pendurou-a acima do céu

E disse o magistrado estúpido para olhar para o céu

O plenilúnio estava pendurado acima do céu

A Primeira Vez Senhor Lee Foi Enganado

Senhor Lee sempre jactou que
Ele nunca tinha sido enganado por alguém toda a sua vida
Um dia de inverno muito frio, um amigo veio visitá-lo
E disse-lhe, "Eu vi uma cereja do tamanho de uma melancia
Em uma cerejeira no meu caminho aqui."

Depois de ouvir isso, Senhor Lee disse,
"Não há tal coisa como uma cereja do tamanho de uma melancia.
Eu não vou ser enganado por isso. Eu nunca vou ser enganado
por isso!"
Mas o amigo disse,
"Eu vi com meus próprios olhos!
Eu até vi uma cereja do tamanho de um melão."

Depois de ouvir isso, Senhor Lee disse,
"Não há tal coisa como uma cereja do tamanho de um melão.
Eu não vou ser enganado por isso. Eu nunca vou ser enganado
por isso!"
Seria crível se era

O tamanho de um pêssego ou uma ameixa."

Depois, o amigo falou,

"Você realmente nunca foi enganado por alguém antes?

Então eu enganei você pela primeira vez.

Como seria uma cereja crescer neste inverno gelado?

Ha-ha-ha!"

E riu alto. Ele riu abertamente.

Montanha Baekdu e a Montanha Halla

Há muito, muito, muito tempo atrás

Vovô Baekdu

Comeu jujubas

E sempre jogou as sementes

Para um lugar

As sementes empilharam e empilharam

E tornou-se uma montanha

Desde então,

Pessoas nomeou a montanha depois do vovô

E chamou-lhe Montanha Baekdu

Há muito, muito, muito tempo atrás

Vovô Halla

Sempre jogou pedras de Badoog[35]

Para um lugar

Toda vez que a terra e o mar foram revertidos

---

35) Um jogo de tabuleiro Coreano como o xadrez

As sementes empilharam e empilharam

E tornou-se uma montanha

Desde então,

Pessoas nomeou a montanha depois do vovô

E chamou-lhe Montanha Halla

Jactando Suas idades

Era uma vez,

O tigre, a raposa, e o sapo

Cada argumentou que

Eles eram mais velhos do que o outro

O tigre disse primeiro, "Eu nasci em tempos antigos

Do imperador japonês."

Depois, a raposa disse, "Eu nasci durante

O governação do Shennong[36]."

Mas o sapo não disse nada

E verteu grossos pingos de lágrimas

O tigre e a raposa

Disseram para o sapo,

"Então você esta chorando porque

Você nasceu última, certo?"

---

36) Shennong, também é conhecido como o *Imperador dos cinco grãos*, foi um
lendário imperador da China e herói

Mas o sapo disse a eles,

"Isso absolutamente não e a razão.

Estou chorando porque

Lembrei-me de repente

O meu filho mais velho

Quem nasceu em tempos antigos

Do imperador japonês

E meu segundo filho

Quem nasceu no

Governação do Shennong

Depois de ouvir o sapo falar,

O tigre e a raposa estavam vergonhosos

Para se jactar suas idades

Em frente do sapo

E imploraram por misericórdia e disseram,

"Vovô sapo,

Por favor perdoe-nos,

Por favor perdoe-nos."

O Servente do Oficial Senhor Kim do Andong

O oficial Senhor Kim quem viveu em Andong,
Estava indo para Seul com seu servente
Ele ficou com muito fome
E disse ao seu servente para ir comprá-lo
Uma tigela de sopa

O servente comprou a tigela de sopa
Mas ele continuou mexendo nos bolsos
No caminho de volta
Quando Oficial Se nhor Kim pediu-lhe
O que ele estava mexendo nos bolsos,

O servente respondeu,
"Eu deixei cair uma remela na sopa
No meu caminho aqui
E eu estava olhando para ela há alguns momentos.

Mas o óleo parece a remela

E a remela parece muito com o oleo

Portanto, é impossível encontrá-lo.

Isso é terrível!"

Depois de ouvir isso, Senhor oficial Kim

Perdeu seu apetite

E disse ao servente para

Jogar fora a sopa

Ou comê-la

Ou fazer o que quiser

Depois de ouvir isso, o servente pensou,

"Sim! Eba!"

E comeu a tigela de sopa em um instante

Eu Também Sou Um Castanheiro

O professor Lee Yulgok do dinastia Joseon
Estava destinado a ser mordido por um tigre
Alguém disse uma vez, "Se você planta mil
Castanheiros, você não vai ser mordido por um tigre.
Então sua família havia plantado mil castanheiros

Mas um dia, enquanto Lee Yulgok estava jogando sozinho em
casa,
Um tigre veio e disse, "Vamos contar juntos quantas
Castanheiros estão plantadas em sua casa!"

Uma árvore, duas árvores, três árvores
Eles contaram as árvores juntos
Quando alguma coisa grande aconteceu
Havia apenas 999 castanheiros
Houve exatamente uma árvore
Faltando das 1000 árvores

O tigre abriu bem sua boca e disse,

"Como há um castanheiro faltando

A partir das árvores plantadas aqui,

Eu vou te comer!"

E atacou o Professor Lee Yulgok

Mas naquele momento, Professor Lee Yulgok acenou seus mãos

e disse,

"Olha! Eu também sou um castanheiro! Eu também sou um

castanheiro!"

Depois de ouvir isso, o tigre disse,"

"Ah ok! Então há exatamente mil árvores! Há 1000 árvores!"

E voltou-se para as montanhas

O Homem Que Foi Escolhido Como o Administrador

Muito tempo atrás, em uma aldeia em Daegu,

O novo magistrado veio de Seul

E quatro pessoas se ofereceu para ser o administrador

O novo magistrado contemplou em quem

Ele deve escolher como seu administrador

E decidiu que iria escolher aquele quem

Podia adivinhar sua pergunta difícil

Como seu administrador

O novo magistrado contemplou e contemplou

E fez uma pergunta,

"Quantas montanhas estão aqui em Daegu?"

Senhor Lee respondeu, "Isso é mais do que eu posso responder

Porque há mais de uma ou duas montanhas aqui."

Senhor Kim respondeu, "Há a montanha Palgong, a montanha Biseul,

E a montanha Duryu."

Senhor Park respondeu, "Há uma grande montanha

e uma pequena montanha."

E por ultimo, Senhor Hong respondeu, "Há um
total de quatro montanhas em Daegu.

Na primavera, há a montanha de flor,

No verão, há a montanha verde,

No outono, há a montanha de cores outonais

E no inverno, há a montanha branca."

Depois de ouvir o Senhor Hong, o novo magistrad pensou,

'Sim, é isso!' e escolheu o Sr. Hong como seu administrador

Vamos só Comer Bolo de Arroz

Um milionário frugal que não tinha nenhuma ideia
De como fazer um bolo de arroz
Teve uma nora
Um dia, a nora preguntou
Porque ela nunca fez um bolo de arroz
O milionário simplesmente respondeu,
"É só uma perda para fazer um bolo de arroz."

Depois de ouvir o milionário,
A nora esponjou três doi[37)] de arroz
Em frente do milionário
E joeirou o arroz para que se parecia
Havia seis doi de arroz
E mostrou para o milionário novamente

---

37) Uma medida seca coreana

vDepois de olha-lo, o milionário frugal disse,

"A final, eu acho que não é uma perda

Para fazer um bolo de arroz.

Minha querida, vamos fazer um bolo de arroz.

Vamos fazer um bolo de arroz."

A nora fez um bolo de arroz adicionando

purê de feijão e deu o bolo a milionário frugal

O milionário frugal comeu o bolo de arroz e disse,

"Não vamos comer arroz mais.

Querida, vamos só comer bolo de arroz.

Vamos só comer bolo de arroz.

É tão delicioso e além disso,

Não há nenhuma perda fazendo esse bolo.

Vamos só comer bolo de arroz."

A Nora Muda

Há muito tempo atrás, quando uma senhorita
Foi se casar, o pai dela admoestou a ela
dizendo, "Querida, quando você é casado,
Vive nove anos assim: três anos como uma muda,
três anos como uma pessoa surdam
e três anos como uma pessoa cega."

A senhorita nunca falou depois que ela se casou
Ela só falou em gestos
O sogro não aguentar a nora mais
y chamou seus serventes
E disse-lhes para levá-la de volta para seus pais

Os serventes levaram a senhorita
Em uma liteira volta para seus pais
Mas enquanto eles passaram por um pinhal
Eles deixá-la sair da liteira
Para que ela pudesse fazer xixi

Ela viu um faisão sentado no bosque de pinheiros

E disse, "Eu gostaria de poder pegar o faisão

E fazer um prato de acompanhamento

E servir meu sogro."

Depois de ouvir isso, os serventes levaram ela na liteira denovo

E levou-a de volta para seu sogro

E disseram-lhe que ela falou

Ele tornou-se muito satisfeito e começou a dançar

Dançou com muito alegria

O Coelho

Um caçador foi caçar e viu um coelho
E atirou o coelho na perna com uma arma
O coelho correu mancando

Um cão estava andando pela trilha da montanha
Quando ele viu o coelho correndo com um manco
Ele correu para-lo e mordeu-lo
E levou para casa

O caçador seguiu o cão arfando e bufando
Havia apenas uma criança de sete anos
Dentro da casa

O caçador disse a ela para
Dar de volta o seu coelho
E a menina disse escrupulosamente,
"A pessoa que fez a perna do coelho mancado e você
mas foi com certeza o meu cão que pegou o coelho

E já que você precisa a pele de coelho e

Meu cão precisa a carne

Você pode ter a pele de coelho e

Nós vamos dar o meu cão a carne de coelho."

As Pessoas Que Eram Parcialmente Surdas

Há muito tempo atrás, em uma casa no distrito de Gyeongsang
Vivia uma nora parcialmente surda,
Uma sogra parcialmente surda, e um servente parcialmente surdo

Um dia, a nora estava na cozinha
E disse que ia fazer café da manhã
E começou a preparar pratos de acompanhamento
Enquanto batendo a tábua de cortar

A sogra nem sequer ouviu o som claramente
E disse desde o dormitorio,
"Querida, o que você está dizendo?
Não coloque a culpa em mim!"

A nora nem sequer ouviu a sogra claramente
E disse desde a cozinha,
"Você está repreendendo a mim denovo hoje
Para algo que aconteceu há três dias!"

O servente nem sequer ouviu a nora claramente

E disse desde o patio,

"Você ainda está me repreendendo

Por quebrar o penico acidentalmente há dois meses!"

O Professor da Escola da Aldeia

O professor de escola da aldeia estava ensinando

A cartilha de caracteres chineses

Mas não importa o quanto ele ensinou o estudante estúpido

O estudante não entendia

Então, o professor disse calmamente o estudante,

"Eu acho que seria melhor para você vender peixe em vez de

estudar.

Vai para grande lugares que tem muitas pessoas e só fala, 'compra

peixe!'"

O estudante estúpido fez como lhe foi dito

E foi para um grande local com muitas pessoas e falou, "Compra

peixe!"

Mas esse lugar era uma reunião para lamentar a perda de um

homem velho

Pessoas ficou raiva e repreendeu o ele,

"Onde você acha que você está vendendo peixe!"

O estudante estúpido foi para seu professor e lhe disse,

"Eu só fiz como você disse e foi repreendido."

Depois de ouvir o estudante, o professor

Afagou o estudante nos ombros e disse-lhe calmamente de novo,

"Quando você vai para lugares assim,

Você tem que primeiro perguntar às pessoas,

'Está bem?'"

O estudante estúpido falou, "Muito bem, senhor." E foi

Para um grande lugar com muitas pessoas, e preguntou as

pessoas,

"Está bem?"

Mas era um lugar para celebrar o 70º aniversário de um homem

velho

Pessoas ficou raiva e repreendeu o ele,

"Onde você acha que você está perguntando às pessoas se eles

estão bem!"

O Filho do Bilionário e A Filha do Milionário

Um dia, o bilionário

Preguntou sua nora,

Quem era a filha do milionário

"Você sabe como preparar a mesa?"

"Eu não sei, senhor."

"Você sabe como tecer roupa de linho?"

"Eu não sei, senhor."

"Você sabe como costurar roupas?"

"Eu não sei, senhor."

Quando alguem preguntou alguma coisa,

Ela sempre disse,

"Eu não sei, eu não sei."

Um dia, o milionário

Preguntou seu genro,

Quem era o filho do bilionário

"Você sabe juntar lenha nas montanhas?"

Ele imediatamente foi para as montanhas

E voltou com uma carga de árvores

"Você sabe como fazer sandálias de palha?"

Ele imediatamente fez um par de sandálias

"Você sabe como cortar lenha?"

Ele imediatamente cortou uma pilha de lenha

Não havia nenhum trabalho que ele não consegui fazer

Não havia nada que ele não consegui fazer

As Cigarras da Montanha Seorak

Um longo, longo tempo atrás, não havia cigarras

Em Montanha Seorak

Porque há tantas cigarras agora?

É porque todos eles vieram de Ulsan

Havia um taoísta vivendo em Ulsan

E tudo o que fez durante o dia inteira

Era comer e dormir

Um verão, as cigarras

Estavam chorando muito alto

Que o taoísta não conseguia dormir

Então ele decidiu fazer as cigarras calar

E tentou amaldiçoá-los e soprar todas as cigarras

Mas as cigarras eram muito astutos

E sentiram o que o taoísta ia fazer

Eles voaram todo o caminho para Montanha Seorak

Para evitar a maldição

E desde esse dia,

Havia cigarras vivendo em Montanha Seorak também